Willow stared out at the night sky and wondered what the future had in store.

"I thought you might still be awake."

She hadn't heard the door open, but she heard the husky-voiced drawl and spun around to stare in disbelief. "Get out of my room," she snapped, but as she watched, Theo closed the door softly behind him and turned the key. "Haven't you done enough damage for one day?" she said bitterly.

"Be quiet." He moved towards her. He was wearing only a short toweling robe that exposed his broad chest and long legs.

All arrogant Greek male, cold fury glittered in his dark eyes. He allowed no one to disrespect him—man or woman—and certainly not this woman.

"You owe me, Willow, eight long years, and now is my time to collect."

Harlequin Presents®

GREEK TYCOONS

They're the men who have everything— except a bride....

Wealth, power, charm—
what else could a handsome tycoon need?
In THE GREEK TYCOONS miniseries you
have already met some gorgeous Greek
multimillionaires who are in need of wives.

Now it's time to meet the incomparable Theodore
Kadros in Jacqueine Baird's

The Greek Tycoon's Love-Child

This tycoon is determined to reclaim
his woman and child...*whatever* it takes!

Jacqueline Baird

THE GREEK TYCOON'S LOVE-CHILD

GREEK
TYCOONS

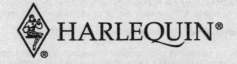

HARLEQUIN®

TORONTO • NEW YORK • LONDON
AMSTERDAM • PARIS • SYDNEY • HAMBURG
STOCKHOLM • ATHENS • TOKYO • MILAN • MADRID
PRAGUE • WARSAW • BUDAPEST • AUCKLAND

ISBN 0-373-12422-8

THE GREEK TYCOON'S LOVE-CHILD

First North American Publication 2004.

www.eHarlequin.com

Printed in U.S.A.

CHAPTER ONE

THEODORE KADROS paid the cab driver. It was a warm June evening and he shrugged off his jacket as he walked up to the open front door of the Georgian terraced house in the centre of London Mayfair. It was a small asset in the vast family-owned international property company. The house had been used over the past few years by his sister, Anna, who was currently sharing with three other students from University College London. He had known all of the girls, but one of them, Liz, had left a month ago, and he had yet to meet her replacement.

A wry smile twisted his firm lips. The new girl was obviously not averse to partying. It was Friday night and the place was lit up like a Christmas tree, a party in full swing. He walked into the hall, hooked his jacket on the wall stand, avoided one or two couples in clinches and headed for the living room. The music was loud and the laughter louder. Anna wasn't expecting him until Monday and she was obviously making the most of her last weekend without her older brother breathing down her neck.

The way he felt at the moment, he did not blame her. After five weeks attending to business in South America he had flown into New York yesterday looking forward to spending a long weekend with his girlfriend of the past ten months, Dianne, a high-flying New York lawyer. Tired and in need of relaxation, Theo had arrived only for Dianne to give him the spiel: *Where was their relationship going? Couldn't they just curl up and talk for this evening?*

After a lot of talk, he had curled up eventually in the

guest bedroom... And it was Theo who'd said 'No' in the morning. He had been six weeks without her and consequently without sex. He was always monogamous as long as a relationship lasted, but, lovely as Dianne was, no way would he let her, or any woman, manipulate him using sex. The sound of wedding bells had been so loud in his head, he hadn't been able to get away fast enough.

'Theo. What are you doing here?' Anna gripped his arm, and looked up at him with shock in her brown eyes. 'I wasn't expecting you until Monday.'

'Have no fear,' he mocked. 'Carry on with the party, just make sure you keep your friends out of my suite.' His sister Anna, at twenty-one, was perfectly capable of looking after herself, but at his father's insistence he was supposed to be keeping a wary eye on her. Their father was Greek and their mother Greek American and, while his mother was a modern woman, his father put great store on traditional Greek values. This was the reason Theo had been loosely based in London for the past three years and kept a room on the top floor of the house. At the family home in Athens Anna led a much more sheltered life than she did in London.

'Sure thing, bro...' Anna resumed dancing with her partner.

Theo helped himself to a stiff whisky, and looked around the neon-lit living room... Not his scene. A glance at his wrist-watch told him it was five minutes to midnight, but unfortunately his body clock was still on American time, and he was not ready to sleep. His hard mouth curled in a cynical smile as he pondered on the vagaries of women. The lovely Dianne in particular.

Dianne had known the score from the beginning. She was a beautiful, intelligent, career-minded lawyer, just the type he liked, and yet within a few months she had been after a wedding ring. But she had picked the wrong man with him. He was a bachelor and intended to stay that way for the foreseeable future.

He glanced around the crowded room. At the end of July Anna would be finished at university. Then the house would be converted into business premises, which had been the original intention when the family firm had bought the place. But when Anna had insisted she wanted to live in student accommodation, their father had flatly refused. This house had been a compromise between father and daughter. Still, looking around now, at the assorted party guests writhing in what looked like a mass fertility dance, Theo could understand his father's point of view.

At the same time he realised he wouldn't mind a writhing body of the female persuasion beneath his own for the night, but he wasn't into one-night stands, and certainly not with his sister's friends. It was a bit too close to home. Turning, he threaded his way through the crowd. A cup of coffee was what he needed, not more whisky, and he made his way to the kitchen.

He pushed open the door and walked in, closing it behind him. Turning, he stopped dead. In all of his twenty-eight years he had never seen anything like her...

The woman was standing with her back to him, pouring a bottle of some garishly coloured liquid down the sink. Her hair was as black as midnight and flowed in silken waves almost to her waist. An expanse of smooth pale flesh revealed the feminine flare of her hips and a black band that only just passed for a skirt covered high, firm buttocks. And her legs... Theo drew in a harsh breath and shoved a hand in his trouser pocket; he had not been so quickly or so shockingly aroused since he had been a testosterone-fuelled schoolboy. Her legs went on for ever...long and shapely and as pale as alabaster.

'Well, hello,' he drawled throatily. He wasn't faking the huskiness in his tone; her rear view alone took his breath away as he quickly covered the space between them.

Willow dropped the bottle in the sink at the sound of the deep masculine voice and spun around. Her lips parted but no sound came out. Walking towards her was the most beautiful man she had ever seen. Tall and casually dressed in softly pleated cream trousers and a blue buttoned-down shirt, he was big and bronzed and radiated energy like an electrical storm. Straight black hair was cut in a well-groomed, if slightly long, style that gave him a raffish air.

He was every teenage romantic fantasy rolled into one. The slow, intimate curl of his lips as he smiled made her heart race out of control and her stomach flutter in the most alarming way. For a moment time stood still and she was completely disorientated.

She had read about the thunderbolt of love at first sight, but had doubted it existed. Then her eyes met his and she saw her own reflection in the dark liquid depths and knew that it was true. Her eyes widened and a frisson shivered through her body as she thought he saw through to her soul, so intense was the connection.

She heard him speak but her breath locked in her throat and she was incapable of making a response. She simply stared, excitement sizzling through her. She had never felt like this in her life before; it had to be love, she thought impulsively. What else could it be? Later, much later, she would realise her mistake...

When the woman turned around Theo was shocked. Brilliant blue eyes blazed into his but the eyes were ringed with thick black kohl and even thicker mascara. Garish blue eye-shadow coated her heavy lids and her mouth was a gash of red. Her face, heavily covered in make-up, was a complete contrast to her pale skin tone.

Her shoulders were bare and as pale as her legs. His gaze dropped lower to the soft curve of pert breasts, which were blatantly displayed by her metallic silver bra, and lower still to her flat stomach and the indentation of her navel, which the apology for a skirt she wore could not hide. Then he saw the jewel in her belly button and he gulped. Bad make-up aside, the woman was sex on legs.

'A beautiful girl like you should not be hiding in the kitchen,' he said, stopping a foot away. 'I am Theo Kadros, Anna's brother, and you are…?' He paused and held out his hand. He noticed that her eyes were even more incredibly blue close up and he thought they could not possibly be real. But right at that moment he didn't care; it was her body that was driving him crazy. As the pause lengthened she simply stared at him and he added, 'Are you staying here now?' Maybe she was the new student. 'Or have I conjured you up in my imagination, a legendary Mycenaean beauty,' he teased, 'and you can't speak?' He smiled, her fabulous eyes widened and she blinked.

'My name is Willow, and, yes, I am staying here,' said a cool polite voice. A slender elegant white hand was formally held out to his. He took it and her touch electrified him.

'Your name suits you,' he drawled throatily, his dark eyes sweeping down her shapely body. His iron-clad rule not to get involved with Anna's house mates flew right out of the window. 'So will you dance with me, Willow?'

'I don't think I can,' she said, her voice soft and low. 'Not the way they are in there.' And she tilted her head towards the door, her long, silken hair gliding over one shoulder with the gesture.

'Then let me teach you my way,' Theo murmured, and he didn't just mean dance. Beneath the ton of make-up her features were even, her nose small and straight, her lips full and luscious. In fact she was quite stunningly beautiful, he thought. He wanted her with a hunger that was turning him inside out. The fact that she appeared to have no dress sense faded into insignificance. His body had taken over his mind and he didn't give a damn.

He held her in his arms, ignoring the frenzied antics of the other dancers, and she flowed against him as if she were made for him. He buried his head in her glorious hair and it smelt of fresh apples. She had a unique personal scent like no perfume he had ever known. Their conversation was limited because of the noise of the music, but he did discover she was studying English. He made her laugh with his stories and sigh with the subtle caress of his hands against her slender body. Finally, when he asked her to share a drink with him somewhere a little quieter, her hand trustingly in his, she followed where he led.

Opening his eyes, Theo stretched all six feet four of his bronzed body, a contented sigh escaping him. He felt great, better than great—magnificent, and it was all down to the lovely Willow. Immediately he became aroused again. She was his dream woman, and she had fulfilled his every fantasy. He licked his lips. He could still taste her on his tongue, feel the perfect rose-tipped nipples filling his mouth, and the exquisite length of her long legs wrapped around his hard body. The amazing tightness of her sheathing him. Her keening little cries when they'd climaxed together, and her eager, if somewhat surprised, response when he had led her slowly into ever more erotic ways of making love. If she had not been so wildly responsive he might have thought she had never had a man before.

Yes, breaking up with Dianne was the best thing he had ever done. Willow was much more to his liking. A perfect replacement. He rolled onto his side, reaching for her, and then he realised the bed was empty. She was probably in the bathroom. At one point last night she had briefly left him and had returned with her face washed clean of make-up. Theo had been stunned by her natural beauty and had taken her all over again.

Thinking about it now, he threw back the sheet, swung his long legs off the bed, and stood up, his magnificent body fully aroused. Then he remembered—she wouldn't be in the bathroom. He felt almost like a teenager again, a broad, anticipatory grin illuminating his handsome face.

As the light of dawn had filtered into the bedroom, Willow had eagerly agreed to his suggestion to spend the weekend with him, but not under the curious eyes of his sister. He had agreed and let her slip back to her own room to get ready, arranging to meet her downstairs at nine. Theo was sure the rest of the house mates would still be asleep after the party and they could slip away unnoticed.

Although the thought of sharing a shower with Willow held great appeal, the thought of the days, and nights, ahead held even more. He cast a reminiscent smile back at the rumpled bed, saw the blood stain and froze...

Oh, hell! She couldn't possibly have been a virgin? No. He shook his dark head dismissing the notion. It wasn't possible, not dressed the way she had been last night. Or the fact that she had fallen into bed with him within an hour of their meeting. Anyway, Anna had told him that the new girl was doing a postgraduate course so she had to be at least twenty-two. There must be another explanation for it. He glanced around the room, and only then did he register the time: eleven o'clock. Oh, hell! He cursed again; he had overslept for the first time in years. Jet lag had obviously caught up with him—that and his energetic love-making with Willow most of the night.

Dashing into the shower, he told himself not to panic.

After the marvellous night they had shared she would still be waiting for him downstairs, he was sure. Theo's head was full of plans to introduce the beautiful Willow to all the finer things in life, himself included. He would be her style guru and take her to the best beauticians and dress her in designer gowns so she could truly fulfil her magnificent potential.

Five minutes later, dressed in denim jeans and a black polo shirt, he strolled confidently into the kitchen. Anna and her two friends, Maggie and Jo, sat at the table. A fourth, blonde girl whom Theo had never met before was also seated. She must be a hanger-on from the party, he assumed.

'Hello, Theo. Sleep well?' Anna greeted him. 'Sit down and I'll get you a coffee—you look as if you need it.'

Doing as she said, he joined them at the scrubbed pine table and listened in to their post-mortem on the night before. Finally, after drinking a second cup of Anna's strong brew, he asked the question that was uppermost in his mind, hopefully without raising his sister's suspicions. 'So where is your new tenant? I think she said her name was Willow. Tall with black hair. I met her in the kitchen last night.'

All four girls started to laugh and the blonde answered. 'I'm the new tenant, Emma. You must mean The Mole, and she's gone.'

Disappointment hit him like a punch in the stomach, and he wanted to yell, *Gone where?* But, hiding his shock at the information, Theo queried lightly, 'The Mole? Why do you call her that?' Willow had lied to him. She was not the new student in the house, and she had obviously left without saying a word to him. He told himself not to worry—after all, Anna and her friends knew who she was. With a bit of careful questioning it should not be too hard to find out where Willow was and get her back, and he wanted her back.

'She and I attended the same convent boarding-school together. It was popular with families in the Foreign and Commonwealth Office. The Mole was Willow's nickname,' Emma answered. 'Think *Wind in the Willows* and with a name like Willow and all that black hair, it was obvious. She was much smaller then and had her head buried in a book all the time, so the name sort of stuck, I suppose. She was four or five years behind me, and never had much to say. I don't really know her all that well. We tried our best to get her involved last night but without much luck; she vanished about midnight to her room.'

Theo stilled. Not her room, his. The mention of a convent school made him feel decidedly queasy. But Theo did not betray what he was thinking. 'She didn't look much like a mole to me, with a jewel in her belly and a skirt that barely covered her buttocks,' he drawled sardonically.

The laughter erupted again and this time Anna answered. 'Well, it was a Tarts and Vicars party, not that you would notice, Theo.'

'A Tarts and Vicars...' he repeated, his darkly handsome face creasing in a frown. 'You mean you deliberately dressed up like tarts?' he asked angrily, amazed that his own sister could be so dumb. Surely she knew what kind of signal scanty clothes sent out to the male sex.

'Yes.' Anna grinned at him. 'But that doesn't mean we are. So you can get your older-brother disapproving scowl off your face.'

The trouble was, Theo realised belatedly, he had reacted with just such a baseless foundation last night when he had seen the lovely Willow, and he wasn't proud of the fact.

'As for The Mole... Willow Blain,' Emma amended when he shot her a dark glance, 'I did my best to get her involved and lent her a stick-on belly-button gem and some of my clothes so she would blend in, but—' she glanced down at her own body, and then flirtatiously back at Theo '—as you can see I'm quite small and I could not believe how tall Willow had grown in the years since we last met.'

Theo's memory summoned up all too vividly Willow's tall, lithe body. The brilliant blue eyes and skin as smooth as silk, and his body immediately reacted with shocking enthusiasm. But his incisive brain also reminded him of the face scrubbed free of make-up, and the stained bed, and just as quickly his heated response was quenched. Anger and confusion raged though him, the latter emotion not one he was familiar with. When he could trust his voice he asked abruptly, 'So Willow is not at university with you?' He rose to his feet. Theo suddenly had a horrible premonition he was not going to like what he was about to hear.

'Good heavens, no,' Emma said with a giggle. 'She was only here because my father has known Mrs Blain for years; she is employed by the diplomatic corps and is in India at the moment. Anyway, my dad asked if we could put Willow up for the night, because her mother did not like the idea of her being on her own in a London hotel, especially as it was her eighteenth birthday. She only left school yesterday and she had to catch a flight out of Heathrow this morning to join her mother.'

'Why are you so interested, Theo?' Anna asked, her brown eyes, full of merriment, resting on his face. 'Surely you didn't fancy her? Especially when the lovely Dianne has been on the telephone countless times already this morning. I think Willow took the first call before she left and I have fielded the rest. You'd better ring Dianne back; she was beginning to sound frantic.'

Not half as frantic as Theo felt. His stomach churned and he was savagely angry with the four grinning girls, but even more so with himself. Theo could not believe he had been so arrogantly self-centred and had seduced a beautiful, innocent young girl into his bed without a second thought. How could he have been so blind not to have seen that, beneath the appalling make-up and clothes, Willow was barely eighteen.

'Theo,' Anna prompted, 'are you going to ring Dianne?'

'No. We split up, and if she calls tell her I am out.' Glad of the excuse and sick to his stomach, Theo stormed out of the kitchen, and the house.

CHAPTER TWO

SEATED at the circular dining table in a conference room of an exclusive London hotel, Willow wished she could just get up and walk out. Unfortunately her publishing company had insisted she attend. Her third novel, *A Class Act Murder,* had been nominated for the Crime Writer's Prize, and Willow stood a good chance of winning.

More importantly, an appointment had been arranged at five this evening for Willow to meet American producer, Ben Carlavitch, to discuss the proposal of buying the film rights to the book. If by some miracle Willow won the prize it would ensure she got a much better deal.

Three days ago, Willow had been thrilled when Louise, her editor, had informed her about meeting Carlavitch. It had meant staying in London overnight, but excitely she had agreed. However, Willow was now beginning to wish she hadn't bothered.

She glanced around the room full of intense literary people, and felt hopelessly out of place. She had left school at eighteen and had become a writer more by accident than design. She loved reading, especially crime novels, and at the age of twenty she had decided to try to write one. Now, seven years and three books later, she found herself, much against her better judgement, in the spotlight.

The award winner was to be announced after lunch, and Willow wished it were over and done with. She felt pretty certain that she had no hope of winning; the other five nominees were all well-established crime writers.

But two hours later Willow walked out of the conference

room in a daze. She had won. Her acceptance speech was a blur. She had immediately called her son, Stephen, on her editor's mobile and told him the news before being swamped with people wishing to congratulate her.

She still felt weak at the knees with excitement and was grateful for the steadying hand of her editor on her arm as they approached the lift.

'We have to meet our MD and company lawyer in Reception, and then across town to meet Carlavitch. He is really enthusiastic about your book,' Louise said, grinning happily. 'Especially after you winning the award, the publicity will boost our bargaining power immensely. You have it made, Willow. Carlavitch is leaving for Los Angeles later tonight, so we have to make the most of this opportunity, and hopefully secure the deal.'

'What is going on?' Theo Kadros asked the hotel manager as a reporter and cameramen he recognised from the national press hurriedly crossed the foyer. 'You know the company policy: no reporters are allowed to hassle the celebrity guests,' he said curtly.

Theo, as the owner of a multinational company that dealt with property worldwide, including a string of exclusive hotels, had arrived in London this morning on business. As always he was in the process of making a quick inspection of the hotel lobby. Experience had taught him that the unheralded visit gave him a much better idea of how his hotels were being run.

The manager's smile slipped a little. 'Strictly speaking the person in question was not a celebrity when she booked in; no one had ever heard of her. We are hosting the Crime Writer's Prize ceremony lunch, and all the excitement is because the author J. W. Paxton has been announced the winner.'

'Good choice. I read his latest book and thought it was excellent. However, I would hardly have thought the ceremony warranted attention by the national press. It must be a slow news day,' Theo responded.

'Maybe, but then you obviously have not seen J. W. Paxton.' The manager chuckled, his glance swinging to the lift doors opening at the mezzanine level. 'Here *he* comes now, but *he* is a *she*—and what a she! She could double as a model any day. Willow Blain is her real name, apparently.' And he chuckled again.

On hearing Willow's name Theo stiffened and glanced across the crowded foyer to the lift. His dark eyes blazed for a moment, then narrowed on the woman who slowly stepped out. He would recognise that face anywhere. Willow, the woman who had haunted his dreams for nine long years. Now to see her in the flesh again shocked Theo rigid. A sudden anger, fierce and primitive, had him instantly stepping forward, but then just as quickly he stopped himself and stepped back.

He had charged like a bull at the gate the first time he'd met Willow, and lived to regret it. Theo had learned never to make the same mistake twice. His unfinished business with the lovely Willow was private and *very* personal—he could wait...

Casually leaning back against a marble pillar, he studied her with hot dark eyes. The years had been good to her; she had barely changed at all. Her figure a little fuller perhaps, but she was still sex on legs. The eager faces of the male reporter and photographer proved it, he thought angrily as his glance skidded over them.

The fact that she was a successful crime writer surprised him, and then with a wry smile he thought again. Emma had called her The Mole, not just because of her name, but because she was quiet and always had her head buried in a book. Perhaps it was not that unusual that she would choose to write, but as a man—now that was unusual.

The book he had read, *A Class Act Murder,* had appealed to him because the plot had been strong and had tested the intelligence of the reader. The writing style of the author was full of vigour and passion. The passion of Willow he could personally vouch for, and as for the intrigue, well, she had certainly fooled him the first time they had met.

For a moment the sudden camera flash blinded Willow and she was completely unaware of the tall, dark-haired man's silent scrutiny of her as she exited the lift.

'What was that for?' she asked Louise, blinking furiously. 'I thought the man at the lunch was the official photographer from the *Crime Writers' Review.*'

Louise chuckled. 'Yes, but the fact that J. W. Paxton is actually a woman, and the fact that Carlavitch is interested in buying the film rights, make it a much bigger story. Obviously, the news has already reached the nationals.' Louise grinned up at Willow. 'And let's face it, Willow, you are pretty gorgeous.'

'I wish I'd stayed a man,' Willow muttered darkly, walking by Louise's side towards the shallow flight of stairs that led down to the reception.

'Hold it there, Willow,' the photographer shouted, and the two women halted a couple of steps from the foyer.

Straightening her slender shoulders, Willow flicked a tendril of black hair from her cheek and tried to appear relaxed. She wished she had not left the jacket that matched the mint-green dress she was wearing in her room. She was suddenly terribly conscious that the heart-shaped neckline revealed more of the upper curve of her breasts than she was happy with. The rest of the dress fitted smoothly over her shapely figure but the skirt ended two inches too far above her knee for Willow's liking. Living in Devon, and, until recently, undecided whether to attend the awards ceremony, it was the best thing she'd been able to find to wear at the last minute.

Her hair had started the day severely tied back with a matching silk scarf but had now begun to escape, tendrils softly curling around her face and her elegant neck. Hot and flushed from the excitement and the attention, she still managed to stand tall and face the numerous questions the reporter fired at her.

Louise raised her voice. 'Right, that is enough, gentlemen, we have a very important meeting at five so—'

'One more shot, Willow, please,' the photographer shouted. 'How about this time with your hair loose and leaning forward over the stair rail, with a hand on your hip?' he suggested with a cheeky grin.

Willow blushed scarlet and, laughing, said, 'No way.' She was a writer not a pin-up and her initial pleasure in actually winning the award was now fast diminishing. It suddenly dawned on her that it probably wasn't the best idea in the world to have her picture featured in the national press. One never knew who might see it, and she valued her privacy above all else. She lifted her hand and brushed past the pushy photographer, and froze.

A head taller than every other man in the hotel, he wore a pale grey suit that fitted his broad shoulders to perfection and loosely followed the line of his great torso. He moved with a lithe grace for such a big man, and he was moving towards her... Theo Kadros... She could hardly believe her own eyes. Frozen in shock, she simply stared. A ghost from the past—but unfortunately all too real. It was *Theo*.

His black hair was streaked with silver now and if anything he was more stunningly handsome, more powerfully masculine than she had ever allowed herself to remember.

His eyes gleamed black as night and were fringed with thick curling lashes that any woman would kill for. Willow now noticed that his eyes were fixed on her, with a disturbing intensity. She silently groaned. Seeing Theo again was all she needed at this point to turn what little shred of delight she had in winning the award to dust. But even so she could not tear her eyes away from his. It was a replay of the first time they'd met—she was dumbstruck.

'I think Miss Blain has answered enough of your questions.' Theo's strong hand quickly curved around her elbow, and Willow found herself being marched across the foyer and straight into a large office.

'You.' Willow finally found her voice, and glanced wildly around—they were in the manager's office! 'We can't come in here,' she said inanely.

'We can when I own the hotel,' Theo Kadros declared arrogantly. Turning to the startled manager, he said, 'Get out there and get rid of those two news hounds. Reassure Miss Blain's publisher that she won't be a minute, and shut the door behind you when you leave.'

'No,' Willow said shakily. This could not be happening to her. Wide blue eyes fixed in horror now on his hard, handsome face, she felt a slither of fear slowly trickling down her spine.

She had convinced herself over the past nine years that she would never see Theo Kadros again. Now standing in front of him she wondered what the odds were of them bumping into each other like this. Probably astronomical! This had to be the most disastrous coincidence of all time, and instantly Willow realised the consequences could be catastrophic.

It was so unfair; at her moment of triumph, Theo Kadros had appeared like a spectre at the feast. What kind of rotten luck was that? she silently screamed. Tearing her gaze from his, she looked around her, terrified he would see the fear and turmoil she knew must be reflected in her eyes.

At their first meeting she had taken one look at him and been utterly entranced by his masculine beauty. Even now, looking back, she inwardly cringed with embarrassment at how very young and innocent she had been.

It had been an unhappy time in her life. Her mother and father had both been in the Foreign Office. Her father had died in an accident in Africa when she was a baby and she did not really remember him. But her mother had continued with her career in the Foreign Office. Willow had spent most of her childhood with her grandmother in Devon. During the holidays Willow would visit her mother at whichever embassy she was attached to, and at the age of twelve she had been sent to boarding-school.

Unfortunately Willow's grandmother had died three months before her eighteenth birthday, and she had been on her way to spend the summer holiday with her mother in India. Alone in London for the first time, and supposedly protected by close friends of her mum, she had been no match for the sophisticated seduction skills of Theo Kadros.

With her only experience of life garnered from books, and her head stuffed full of romantic teenage fantasies, Willow had been instantly mesmerised by the wondrous gleam in his deep dark eyes. And for the first time in her life she had suffered the full force of a man's overwhelming sensual attraction and had been totally captivated. It had been no contest—Willow had surrendered on the spot. She'd fallen head over heels in love with him, and then fallen into bed with him, and had spent a dream-like night making wild, passionate love.

No, not love, sex…Willow instantly amended. She had discovered the true meaning of her Quaker grandmother's many dire warnings about men and sex and their lack of respect *the morning after.*

Like a besotted fool she had believed Theo when he'd asked her to spend the weekend with him, so they could get to know each other better. She had watched him fall asleep and then returned to her room and packed. Later, feeling every inch a real woman, she had slipped downstairs to ring her mother to tell her of her change of plan. Her head had been full of love and happy ever after. But before she'd had a chance to call the telephone in the hall had rang.

Politely answering, she had listened in numb disbelief as a woman called Dianne had asked to speak to her boyfriend, Theo Kadros. Shocked into answering honestly, Willow had said he was still in bed asleep. The woman had hesitated for a moment, and then laughed, saying, 'He is probably tired because I kept him up till dawn the night before. Don't bother waking him; I am flying over today, and I want him rested for tonight.' She had then instructed Willow to inform Theo as soon as possible that his fiancée had called.

Anna had appeared as Willow had slowly replaced the receiver, and had asked who had called. Willow had told her that it was Theo's fiancée, and had had the horrible truth confirmed when Anna had replied, 'Dianne, you mean.'

Even then Willow had not wanted to believe what she'd been hearing. She had hated herself but she hadn't been able to help questioning Anna. She had asked her if Theo had known Dianne very long, and had been mortified when Anna had informed her about a year, which was a record for her brother. Anna had explained that this was probably because Dianne was prepared to put up with his playboy

lifestyle, but had added that their dad had been grumbling
lately that it was time Theo settled down.

The final nail in the coffin for Willow had been when
Anna had confirmed that Theo had just flown in late last
night after visiting Dianne in New York. Willow had not
needed to hear any more. She'd realised what a complete
and utter fool she had been, and half an hour later she had
been in a taxi heading for the airport.

Now, nine years later, she looked back up into his darkly
attractive face and her blue eyes clashed with gleaming
black. For a moment the breath left her lungs as she realised
he was watching her with cold, almost angry scrutiny. Even
so, she could not prevent the sudden acceleration of her
pulse rate and the sick twist of sensual hunger that tied her
stomach in knots.

'What exactly do you think you are doing?' she asked
in a voice that was not quite steady. Hating the ease with
which he had affected her all over again, Willow took a
couple of steps back.

'Rescuing an old friend.' His dark eyes narrowed on her
pale face. 'Unless of course you want to pose some more
for those two randy men out there.' He paused, one dark
brow arched sardonically. 'Topless, maybe?' His heavy-
lidded eyes raked slowly over her, taking in the top of her
head, lingering for a moment on the unchanged beauty of
her face and down further, hesitating briefly on the creamy
curve of her breasts revealed by the low neckline of her
dress. 'As I remember, Willow, you certainly have the figure for it.'

She battled back the blush that threatened at his blatant
masculine appraisal. But she could do nothing except pray
that he would not notice the sudden tightening of her nipples against the soft fabric of her dress. 'I didn't need rescuing,' she said, aiming for a firmness she did not feel. 'I

am perfectly capable of looking after myself, thank you. Now, if you will excuse me...I have a meeting to attend.'

'Yes, I heard, with Ben Carlavitch, no less. But first allow me to congratulate you on winning the award. I have read your latest book and thoroughly enjoyed the deviousness of the mind that wrote it. You have certainly done well for yourself.' His dark eyes gleamed appreciatively down into hers, and his firm male mouth curved and softened in a slight smile. 'But then I always knew you had hidden talents,' he drawled silkily.

With maturity Willow had attained a certain degree of sophistication, and she did not deign to acknowledge his obvious innuendo. Theo Kadros was a conceited, arrogant devil. She had once looked up the meaning of his name, Theodore—*Gift of God*, and if ever a man thought he was God's gift it was Theo. Always larger than life, he was a handsome, dynamic man, self-assured to a degree that intimidated most people. Willow knew that she was no exception, but she had no intention of letting him see her fear.

'Thank you,' she said coolly, bravely holding his gaze.

She had read about him over the years; it had been unavoidable. He was incredibly wealthy and had inherited the family business on the death of his father a few years ago. Typically Theo had gone on to quadruple the size of the company. He was feared and respected in equal degrees by the business world, a ruthless, powerful man who had his fingers in many pies. It was just her appalling bad luck that one of the pies happened to be the very hotel she was booked into for the night.

'I am glad you enjoyed the book,' she continued steadily. 'But now, if you will excuse me.' She turned and headed for the door. Meeting Theo Kadros again was her worst nightmare, and she had to get away fast.

'Of course, you have a meeting,' Theo said smoothly,

and moved quickly to open the door, but put a restraining hand on her arm. 'But later, perhaps you would care to join me for dinner?' He paused and added softly, 'Willow?'

The sound of her name on his tongue and his long fingers curved around her bare flesh set every nerve in her body quivering in a sensual response. Mortified at her instant reaction to this man, and calling on every bit of self-control she possessed, she lifted her chin and looked up into his hard face. 'Thank you for the invitation, Theo, but I am afraid I must refuse.'

Theo studied her, his attention wandering from the barely constrained mass of her silken black hair to her brilliant blue eyes. As he watched her he saw the flicker of fear in their sparkling depths. 'You have a husband who might object?' he asked abruptly. Perhaps she was afraid of arousing her partner's jealousy? Theo could understand that. If she were his woman he would not let her out of his sight.

'No...' Willow said without thinking. Then cursed herself for being so honest. Theo had given her the perfect opportunity for her never to see him again and in her panic she had blown it. 'But—' She was going to say she had made other arrangements but never got the chance.

'Good, then there is nothing to stop you joining me.'

The arrogance of the man was astounding. As long as *she* wasn't married it was okay; he had not changed one iota. 'But what about you?' she asked coolly. 'I am sure I read somewhere that you are married. Won't your wife have something to say about you dining with another woman?'

She knew he had married Dianne. It had been in the press a few months after Willow had last seen him. A year or so later there had been a huge article in an international magazine about Dianne and the villa her husband had built for her in Greece.

'I doubt it,' Theo answered. 'We were divorced years ago.'

Dianne had probably found out what a two-timing louse he was, Willow thought dryly.

'So what do you say, Willow? We are both free and single, so there is nothing to stop us spending the evening together. We can catch up on old times.'

'Sorry.' She tried a brief smile and explained, 'But I have already arranged to have dinner with my editor, so no, thank you.' She reached again for the door handle.

'Then as we are both staying in the same hotel, you must at least join me for a drink later, or I will begin to think that I have upset you in some way,' Theo drawled in his deep dark voice. 'Yet, as I recall, we parted with a handshake nine years ago.'

Was she imagining the steely threat present in his soft drawl? She was about to bite back with an angry refusal but thought perhaps it would be wiser to agree. Willow's long lashes lowered slightly over her eyes, masking her expression. One drink and a brief friendly chat before retiring for the night. How hard could that be? She did not dare take the chance of arousing his suspicions. She was returning to Devon in the morning and would never see Theo again. 'Yes, okay, if you are still here when I get back, I'll have a drink with you. But don't spoil your evening waiting for me.' And with this Willow turned and left the office.

Ben Carlavitch was a very handsome man, but to Willow, ensconced in his suite with her publisher, the lawyer and Louise, he could have looked like Quasimodo and she still would not have noticed. She barely registered what was being discussed, and answered yes to everything, heaving a sigh of relief when the rest got down to discussing money.

Her mind was in turmoil. Theo Kadros hadn't changed much in nine years, except he looked harder and more cynical than she remembered him. He was right, they had parted with a handshake, but even now Willow could recall the fierce self-control it had taken to dismiss the man from her life.

Dear God! Thinking about it now, she could not believe she had ever been that young or that naive. The morning after sleeping with Theo she had answered the telephone and all her romantic dreams had gone crashing to the ground. The man whose bed she had just left had been engaged to be married to someone else. He was an unscrupulous fiend; even his own sister had said he was a playboy.

A few hours later, still in a blessedly merciful state of numb shock, Willow had been sitting in the departure lounge at Heathrow Airport waiting for the boarding announcement for her flight. The flight had already been delayed, and Willow had been anxious to get to her mother, and put the shameful events of the previous night behind her. Briefly closing her eyes, she had wondered how she could have been so stupid.

'Willow.'

Her eyes flew open in shock. Theo Kadros was standing in front of her like some dark avenging angel, and she was struck again by his sheer magnetism. But now, in the harsh light of day, the dream-like picture she had of the teasing, tender lover was blasted into oblivion by the ruthless, dynamic power of the man towering over her.

Horrified, she leapt to her feet. She must have been crazy to even think for a minute that a sophisticated man like Theo Kadros could be interested in her for anything but a one-night stand. He was way out of her league, and the bitter realisation gave her the strength to face him. 'What are you doing here?' she asked in a cool, polite voice.

A wry smile curved Willow's full lips as she remembered the look of dismay on Theo's face as his gaze had roamed over her from the top of her head to her toes. She had dressed for comfort for the long-haul flight, in plain white cotton drawstring trousers and a baggy blue sweatshirt. Her hair had been scraped back in two plaits and her face scrubbed free of make-up, and she'd known she'd looked nothing like the glamorous, scantily clad girl he had met the night before.

'I could say…where are we going for the weekend?' he drawled mockingly. 'But then again…' his dark eyes narrowed angrily on her pale face '…perhaps I just came to wish you a happy eighteenth birthday.'

Still in shock, Willow ignored his comment about the weekend and thanked him politely, much to her own amazement.

Stony-faced, he demanded to know why she'd never told him she was so young. She responded petulantly with, You never asked, and he grunted like a wounded bear. He then demanded to know why she had lied to him and let him think she was the new student in the house. Again she told him with quiet reason, 'You asked me if I was staying and I was.'

With his temper rising to boiling point, he pointed out that he would never have slept with her if he had known how young she was, or that she was a virgin. Embarrassed, Willow told him to keep his voice down. Then with a sudden flash of inspiration she informed him that she had simply planned it as something to do when she came of age, adding that she'd thought an older man would be better as he was likely to be more experienced.

His rage barely contained, he demanded how she could treat the loss of her innocence so lightly. He tried to persuade her to keep in touch with him, by telephone or letter, and suggested they meet up again in India, anywhere. When that didn't work he demanded curtly that she keep in touch with him just in case there were any repercussions from the night they had spent together.

Not once did he mention his fiancée, and it was left to Willow to angrily point out, 'Really, Theo, I think you are overdoing it a bit. I bet you didn't say that to the woman who shared your bed the night before me.' She caught the flash of something very much like guilt in his eyes, and knew Dianne had told the truth. Then, with a casualness that pleased her battered heart, she told him he had nothing to worry about, pointing out that he had used protection and that there was always the morning-after pill, implying she had taken one.

At that he stiffened and took a hasty step back, his dark eyes hard and blank. 'Well, then, you are right, there is obviously nothing more to be said.' He made a throw-away gesture with his hand palm up. 'Except I am glad I could be of service,' he drawled mockingly.

At that moment her flight was finally called. 'My flight... No hard feelings, Theo,' she said with a cool smile and took his hand and shook it.

Surprised, he looked at her hand holding his, and then slowly unwound his strong fingers. 'Have a nice life, Willow.' And then he left.

'So what do you think, Willow? Are you agreed?'

Blinking back to the present at just the right time, Willow still couldn't face the anguish she had suffered after Theo had left her that day. 'Yes.' She looked up across the table into the shrewd grey eyes of Ben Carlavitch.

You haven't been listening to anything that has been said.' His handsome face turned into a rueful smile. 'A bit dampening to a Hollywood mogul's ego.' He grinned.

She grinned back. He really was a very attractive man, and about thirty-five, she guessed. 'Yes, I did,' she lied. 'And if my publisher is happy, then so am I.'

'Whoever he is, he is a very lucky man,' he said with a wry smile. 'I just hope he appreciates you. If not, give me a call.'

CHAPTER THREE

THE doorman held open the taxi door and, sliding out, Willow called goodnight to Louise, who was sharing the cab with her. She glanced up at the impressive entrance to the hotel, and shivered slightly in the cool night air. It was almost midnight, and Willow felt sure that Theo Kadros would have given up waiting for her long ago. She certainly hoped so. She had accompanied the others to a smart Italian restaurant after they'd left the meeting with Carlavitch, and had toasted her success with champagne. Willow had deliberately chattered on long after their meal was finished, lingering over the coffee, but finally there had been no alternative but to return to her hotel.

Walking quickly into the lobby, Willow made a beeline for the girl at the reception desk and asked for her room key.

'Thank you.' She almost snatched it from the receptionist's hand in her hurry to get away, and, spinning around, she walked straight into a hard, masculine body. A strong arm closed around her waist, and she slowly lifted her head, her blue eyes clashing with dancing black.

'You don't need to bowl me over, Willow, you did that years ago,' Theo said in a deep, husky drawl, and smiled wickedly down into her startled eyes.

'You're still here,' she blurted. Suddenly conscious of the hard length of his body against her own, Willow took a hasty step back. For a brief second she thought he was not going to release her, but then to her relief his arm fell from her waist and she was free.

Her wary gaze skidded over him. He was wearing an elegantly tailored beige suit with the jacket open. The loosely pleated trousers hung low on his lean hips and faithfully traced his long legs. At some time during the evening he must have discarded his tie as his white silk shirt was open at the neck, revealing the tanned column of his throat and just the slightest hint of black chest hair.

A vivid mental image of her much younger self, leaning over his broad, naked chest teasingly tugging at the tiny black curls, flashed into Willow's mind. She swallowed hard and dragged her gaze back to his face.

'But of course I'm still here, Willow.' His dark eyes captured hers. 'I promised to buy you a drink and talk over old times, and I am a man of my word,' he declared smoothly.

His hypnotic gaze had a paralysing effect on her usually quick brain and before she could refuse a large hand cupped her elbow and she was suddenly walking along by his side. How did he do that? she wondered. She hated this man but one look from him and her senses stirred in inexplicable awareness, the blood instantly flowing quicker through her veins. Disgusted with herself, she snapped, 'It will have to be quick, Theo.'

'Don't worry, the champagne is already on ice.' And with a speed that left her breathless she found herself standing in a lift.

'Wait a minute.' Willow took a step back and came up hard against the rear wall of the suddenly very small box. Theo's hand left her elbow. 'I thought the bar was on the ground floor.'

'The hotel bar is crowded tonight. I thought after the hectic day you have had you would prefer to relax in private,' he explained.

'No, not really,' Willow responded. Private with Theo

Kadros was high up there with her worst nightmare! 'I am rather tired, actually.'

In the close confines of the lift she was intensely aware of him. He was leaning against the wall, his posture relaxed, and the heady scent of his cologne or just the essence of the man teased her nostrils. The effect of his body brushing lightly against her side was having a chaotic effect on her pulse rate. Common sense told her not to antagonise him; the sooner she could escape from his powerful presence, the safer she would feel. 'Perhaps we could have a drink another time.'

'Surely, as an author who plots hair-raising murders of the goriest kind, you cannot be afraid of joining me for a nightcap in my suite?' Theo prompted with the sardonic lift of one dark brow.

'No, of course not,' she denied, and hoped he did not realise she was lying. 'But it is getting late and I really am very tired,' she reiterated.

With a quick glance at the slim platinum watch on his wrist, Theo looked down into her guarded blue eyes. 'Two minutes to twelve. What a coincidence—exactly the same time as when we first met. I don't recall you complaining of tiredness then, Willow. Quite the opposite, in fact.'

All arrogant male sophistication, a sensual smile curved his firmly chiselled lips, inviting her to share the memory. But Willow was not fooled for a minute. She was no longer a silly teenager easily blinded by the sheer animal magnetism of the man, and she responded accordingly.

'Don't remind me.' She tried for a sophisticated smile of her own. 'I try never to dwell on the past but prefer to look to the future.'

He paused as the lift doors opened, splaying his hand on the small of her back and urging her out. 'Then I suppose the possibility of recreating our first meeting, minute by minute, is a no-no,' he said drolly.

'It certainly is,' she snapped, jerking her head back to look up into his darkly handsome face. She saw his teasing expression, and caught the wicked glint of amusement in his dark eyes. For a brief moment he looked years younger, and she was transported back to the night they had met. Remembering his easy humour as he danced with her, talked and joked with her, she could not prevent her lips twitching in a reciprocal smile. She had to give him full marks for nerve and, shaking her head, she shot back with, 'In your dreams, Theo.'

He took out a key and opened the door to his suite, glancing down at her. 'Good, I was beginning to think you had forgotten how to genuinely smile. And don't worry, Willow, I am not going to jump on you. I'm perfectly respectable, almost staid, in my old age. Honest!' He grinned and walked across the room to where an ice bucket stood on a small table. 'Take a seat and let's toast your success, as two old friends should.'

Sinking down onto an over-stuffed sofa, Willow tried to relax. She was a woman with a successful career and perfectly capable of looking after herself, nothing like the impressionable teenager she had once been. She was worrying about nothing; it was just as Theo said—a drink between old friends. Well, not exactly friends, she corrected. They were two people who had spent one explosive night together nine years ago. It still puzzled her why Theo had bothered following her to the airport that day; maybe he had thought it was the polite thing to do, even for someone of his low morals.

She studied him stealthily through the thick veil of her lashes. Light glinted on the silver wings of his thick black hair, highlighting his autocratic profile, a straight blade of a nose, with a square chin and firmly chiselled lips. The intervening years since their first meeting had been good to him. The laughter lines around his gorgeous eyes and the lines bracketing his mouth simply added character to an almost too beautiful face. He had shed his jacket and she noticed how his silk shirt fitted immaculately over his broad shoulders and muscular chest. Narrow-hipped and long-legged, he had the perfect male triangular torso.

He also had the kind of presence and dangerous good looks that made him stand out in any crowd. Add immense wealth and an air of virile masculinity and he was irresistible to the opposite sex…and he knew it. This was why he felt confident enough to joke about his age. Theo would be a handsome devil till the day he died, and the thought of him did nothing for Willow's body temperature.

She watched his brows draw together in concentration as he expertly opened the champagne, and for a second the breath caught in her throat. She had seen the exact same expression on Stephen's face, and suddenly Willow's eyes turned to blue ice. She had been in danger of forgetting just how much of a threat Theo Kadros was to her life. Straightening up in the seat, she held out her hand to take the flute of champagne he offered with a cool smile on her face. 'Thank you.'

The sofa depressed as he lowered his long length down beside her, and, turning slightly, fixed her with his gleaming black eyes. 'To The Mole who turned into a swan.' Willow's blue eyes widened in surprise, and he grimaced slightly. 'My English is not perfect. I think I probably got the phrase wrong. But you know what I mean. Congratulations, Willow.'

Their glasses clinked and she hastily took a sip of the sparkling liquid, forcing herself to keep smiling. There was nothing wrong with his English, and he was perfectly well aware of the fact. So why the pretence? The use of her schoolgirl nickname 'Mole' worried her too. She certainly had not told him about that and it made her wonder just how much Theo actually knew about her.

'So tell me, what made you start writing?'

'Well, as you are obviously aware, my nickname at school was Mole, which I might add I hate. I'm surprised that a man of your intelligence needs to ask any more,' she said dryly.

'Humour me,' he prompted, discreetly refilling their glasses.

Why not? Talking about her work was a much safer subject than reminiscing about their brief past, Willow thought. She told him how she got her first book published, and deftly fielded his questions about where she lived now. She returned the query and asked where he lived. Theo confirmed what she already knew, that he spent most of his time jetting around the world, but that his actual home was in Greece.

'You have a very busy life,' Willow murmured, her blue eyes lifting to his. 'But you seem to thrive on the pressure.'

Theo gave a nonchalant shrug of his broad shoulders. 'I work hard and play hard.' Moving towards her, he casually slid his arm along the back of the sofa behind her, much too close for Willow's comfort.

'Well, your lifestyle would not suit me,' she blurted. The friendly atmosphere between them seemed suddenly fraught with tension. 'I like a quiet life spending time in one place. I don't like travelling.' She knew she was babbling but could not seem to stop. 'I don't like change.' His broad shoulders were angled towards her, and she was starkly aware of the aggressively male body beneath the immaculately tailored silk shirt, and the length of his muscular thigh lightly pressing against her leg.

'I can respect that,' Theo murmured, 'in some instances—for example, your hair.' Willow could not prevent the involuntary jerk of her head as his hand stroked casually over the back of it. 'I am glad you were never tempted to have it cut.'

'Yes, well, my grandmother was very traditional. My mother's job took her all over the world so Grandma virtually brought me up, and she would never dream of cutting my hair. When she was a child her parents were quite strict. They never worked on Sunday, certainly had no television, and the females of the family were not allowed to have their hair cut.'

She stopped and, picking up her glass from the table, she gulped down the rest of the champagne. A foolish thing to do, she realised, because Theo had been quietly topping her glass up. Her brain went into idiot mode when he was around, and nervous tension was making her tell him much more than he needed to know. She glanced up at his handsome face with wary, suspicious eyes. She had to stop rambling on, and get out of here quick before she really let something slip.

'My thanks go to your grandmother. It would be sacrilege to cut such beautiful hair,' Theo murmured and raised a dark sardonic eyebrow. 'But surely, Willow, you aren't trying to tell me that a woman of your age and beauty could be content with all the restrictions your grandmother adhered to? For instance, I am sure there must have been many men in your life since we last met.'

'No. Yes, well...' She faltered, her voice dying away beneath his mocking gaze. Suddenly anger came to her rescue. He had some nerve asking about her love life given he was the world's worst playboy. 'Only one,' she snapped, thinking of her son, Stephen.

Theo gazed down at her with an enigmatic gleam in his dark eyes. 'I'm inclined to believe you.'

'Thanks,' she said with an edge of sarcasm in her tone. In the sophisticated world he inhabited people changed their lovers as often as their clothes. 'But enough about me.' Willow realised that she desperately needed to change the subject, and fast. 'So tell me, what is your sister, Anna, doing now?'

'Ah, yes, Anna,' he said blandly, the gleam of mockery in his gaze. Her blunt attempt to change the subject had been noted, but he was prepared to humour her. 'Anna is now married and the proud mother of two delightful daughters. As their uncle I spoil them rotten, or so Anna tells me.'

Willow immediately knew it had been a big mistake to ask. The sensual tension simmering underneath what she hoped was a cool, attentive expression vanished and she was now flooded with guilt. She had never thought of Theo as the sort of man who would like children. But it was obvious by the softening of his features and the humour in his eyes as he spoke of his nieces that he adored the girls. How much more would he adore his own son?

'You must visit her some time. She will be delighted to see you again.'

'Yes,' Willow said, leaping to her feet. 'Maybe some time, but now I really must go.' The champagne and the companionable chat and, Willow realised, she had been falling under the sophisticated charm of the man all over again. Theo was an enormous threat to her life and she had to remember that.

Theo rose to his feet and placed two hands on her slender shoulders. A disturbing surge of awareness skated down her spine. 'I think Anna always felt a bit guilty she did not do more for your eighteenth birthday. She was under the impression that you left the party early and went to your room because you were bored. I didn't enlighten her,' he concluded with a broad grin, his dark eyes inviting her to share the memory.

Watching his lips part over brilliant white teeth, Willow found herself remembering just how incredible those firm lips had felt on her own mouth and body. She felt heat curl and grow inside her, awakening sensations she didn't want to feel. Mortified by her own instant reaction, she fought back the total body blush that he had aroused in her, with his reminder of just whose room she had shared.

She tilted her chin and bravely held his gaze. But she could do nothing about the long-forgotten sensations that had begun to flare to volatile life inside her. 'Tell Anna from me she has nothing to feel guilty about,' she said, forcing her voice into an approximation of polite concern. 'And, pleasant though the last hour has been, I really see no point in getting in touch with Anna again. We only met the once, and I have never heard from her since. I think it would be better to keep it that way.' And that includes you, she implied, but never said. She wasn't that brave.

Theo was a highly intelligent man—let him draw his own conclusions. She refused to recognise the sudden pang of regret that squeezed her heart. Theo Kadros was banned from her life, however handsome, however tempting, and her own innate honesty forced her to admit, on a purely sexual level, that she was indeed tempted.

'Now you really must excuse me, I—' she began.

'If you thought like that then I am surprised you agreed to have a drink with me,' Theo murmured, his dark eyes narrowing intently on her upturned face. 'And very flattered.' His astute gaze dropped to the lush curve of her mouth and his hands tightened slightly on her shoulders. 'So why did you, I wonder?'

Willow knew she had made an error of judgement. He had a mind like a razor and she had aroused his curiosity. She should have refused his offer the minute she'd seen him and stuck to it. To try and play it cool was one thing, but to give the man the least suspicion she had anything to hide would be fatal. She had to act and act fast.

With a deliberate lowering of her lashes, she allowed her gaze to sweep seductively down his body, lingering for a moment on the hard line of his jaw, before finally levelling to meet his own dark eyes that were now studying her.

'You must know you are a hard man to refuse, Theo,' she said softly. 'I thought there would be no harm in a drink for old times' sake, as you said.' With a smile pinned to her lips, she added, 'Thank you, it has been very nice, but I really must go.'

'Is it all men or just me you are afraid of?' he asked astutely, his responding smile grim. But before Willow could form a reply he suddenly demanded, 'Tell me what really happened to make you run away from me the first time we met? After hearing from Emma about you, seeing you again today, and with the benefit of hindsight, I don't buy your reason you gave me at the airport. I think it is much more likely you were caught by surprise by your own sensuality and got a little more than you bargained for. I think you were running scared, and still are. If I am right, I am sorry.'

Anger simmered inside her, but she managed to keep a smile stuck to her lips. His conceit in his prowess as a lover and his casually given belated apology only served to incense her further. But she forced herself to hide it. Willow knew that if this man ever found out just how much more she had got from him all those years ago, the world would not be a big enough place for her to hide from his fury.

Fear and guilt tamed the furious retort that she would

have liked to have given him, but instead she meekly agreed. 'Something like that, I suppose. But no hard feelings, Theo. And now I really must go.'

'As you wish, but first…' Theo growled softly and pulled her into the hard length of his powerful body. His wide, sensual mouth came crashing down on hers, and, taking advantage of her shocked gasp, he slid his tongue possessively between her parted lips, discovering the moist interior.

For a heartbeat she was frozen in shock, but only for a heartbeat. Twisting, she tried to escape the heady pressure of his mouth. She didn't want this…could not have this… But try as she might she could not escape. Then the hands that had been holding her so firmly against him began sliding over the curves of her body. Willow's eyelids drifted down in helpless response to the exquisite sensuality of his touch, the pressure of his mouth slowly changing. No longer savage, his lips moved skilfully over hers, drugging in their expertise, and a sensation too delicious to be painful clenched her stomach.

Her body betrayed her, exactly as it had done nine years ago, a liquid heat flowing through her veins. She was eighteen again and lost in the wondrous sensations of her first and only love.

His mouth gentled on hers, and shaped it to his own. His tongue sought out the moist dark depths again, and desire fierce and hot surged through her. Willow was instantly overwhelmed in a tidal wave of long-forgotten sensations. No, not forgotten—brutally suppressed to save her sanity. But now the dam was broken. Her slender body arched, pressing into the hard heat of his, her hands reaching to clasp around his neck.

'I want you,' Theo muttered harshly against her mouth. 'God, how I want you.'

The words weren't necessary; she felt it in the pressure of his fiercely aroused body as he moved urgently against her. Her fingers tangled in the silken hair of his head, and her tongue duelled with his in the ever-increasing hunger of their kiss.

Nine long years of celibacy added to the fervour with which she responded to his mouth. Her back arched as he swiftly pulled down the zipper in the back of her dress, and she groaned as for an instant he broke contact. Theo eased her dress down to her waist, and curved an arm around her. His hand splayed up her naked back, and his dark head swooped, his mouth finding hers again. Then with his free hand he found the small clip in the front of her bra.

Willow was drugged by the dark magic of his touch and her head fell back over his arm. She groaned as his fingers trailed over the soft swell of her breast. She opened her dazed eyes, and looked up into burning black, and for a split second she hesitated.

Theo's molten black eyes seared into hers, mesmerising in their intensity. His hand at her back slipped up further and freed the loosely tied scarf so her hair flowed in silken black waves down her back.

'This is how I remember you,' Theo grated, his other hand cupping her breast. His long fingers trailed over the already taut nipple and a devilish gleam of pure male triumph shone in his dark eyes.

'Helplessly aroused and aching.' His fingers plucked at the swollen peak of her breast, sending shafts of sensation from her breast to the apex of her thighs. His night-black eyes blazed triumphantly over her slender milk-white body that arched provocatively over his strong arm. 'Dear God! My memory does not do you justice, Willow. You are more incredibly beautiful than in my wildest dreams, or, I should say, nightmares,' he grated with a trace of bitterness in his tone.

If he had not been holding her she would have collapsed in a puddle at his feet, her body shuddering in an overload of sensation. When he lifted his gaze to hers she saw the savage desire and hunger that he made no attempt to disguise and her heart threatened to burst from her chest.

She tried to speak, but his dark head descended again and brushed surprisingly gently over her softly parted lips. 'I need to taste you again.' he husked. 'Make sure you're real.'

His lips skimmed her throat to fasten hungrily over the rosy peak of one breast. She drew in a sharp, agonised breath, and her hand gripped his shoulder, the other slipping beneath his shirt, trailing over his hot, smooth skin. She felt his reaction in the tiny imperceptible jerk, and then suddenly he was lifting her and pressing her down on the sofa they had just vacated.

'You want me too, Willow.' He stared down at her as he straightened and swiftly shrugged off his shirt.

Her eyes widened on seeing his broad, tanned chest and the dusting of curling black body hair. She ached to touch him, her mouth opened to agree, when Theo broke into the magic world of her senses by speaking again.

'Say it, Willow. I need to hear you say it after our last disastrous one-night stand.'

Her blue eyes focussed on his taut, handsome face and she saw the barely leashed passion in the depths of his hooded eyes. But it was the almost grim smile on his hard mouth that brought sanity to her dazed mind, and squashed the incessant clamouring of her sex-starved body. *Disastrous one-night stand.* The words echoed in her head. Suddenly she was scrabbling to sit up and fasten her bra, dragging her dress up over her shoulders.

Fool…idiot…she castigated herself. What on earth had possessed her? Shame and humiliation flooded through her. Willow went from being flushed with passion to being scarlet-faced with embarrassment. Leaping to her feet, she struggled to zip her dress back up, but her long silken hair got in her way.

'Willow.' A large hand reached for her, and she jumped back.

'No, don't touch me,' she cried, horrified at how easily she had succumbed to his vibrant sophisticated masculine expertise all over again.

'I take it you have changed your mind.' Theo's mocking voice grated over her raw nerves. 'You need to watch that, Willow. Not every man has my self-control,' he drawled cynically. Before she could stop him he spun her around and, lifting the heavy mass of her hair, he zipped up her dress. 'There.' He spun her back to face him, and she cringed, frightened by the grim fury in his black eyes. She knew what she had done was unforgivable. She had led him on and she could not deny it.

'Don't look so terrified,' Theo drawled, almost lazily sweeping the silken tendrils of her hair behind her ears, his hands settling again on her shoulders. 'I have never yet had to force a woman into my bed, and I have no intention of starting with you.'

'Then let go of me,' she said shakily. Willow realised that it would take very little persuasion on Theo's part to have her senseless in his arms again. Her tongue flicked out to moisten her too-dry lips, and she saw the glint in his night-black eyes as he registered her betraying movement.

'Are you really sure, Willow?' he tempted her. 'It is a woman's prerogative to change her mind, and that works both ways,' he opined huskily. His heavy-lidded eyes captured hers, and, mesmerised by the sensual promise in the black depths, she simply stared. 'Perhaps the time wasn't right when we first met. But now we are *both* mature adults, free agents, we won't be harming anyone if we get together again, and I promise you will enjoy the experience.'

His voice was deep and dark, the words rolling off his tongue like melting black chocolate, tempting and almost irresistible. And then he smiled, a slightly crooked twist to his firm lips.

Only one other person she knew smiled like that, especially when he wanted something from her. 'No...no...' She jerked free from his hold. 'No.'

'All right.' Theo shrugged his broad shoulders. 'One "no" will suffice. You said you were tired and I believe you.'

'You do?' she asked stupidly, too dazed to register the cynicism in his tone. She was amazed he was being so reasonable. She knew he was thoroughly aroused and could only marvel at his self-control.

'Yes, but I insist that you join me for breakfast in the morning. What time are you leaving?'

'Well, my train is at ten so I suppose I will leave about nine.' She was too surprised by his reaction to lie.

'Good, then I will meet you in the restaurant downstairs at eight and we can talk then.' Tilting her chin with one long finger, he said, 'Unless you would prefer your breakfast in bed.' Willow gasped and Theo grinned. 'Only teasing. I rushed you last time, and I have no intention of making the same mistake again. I will see you downstairs tomorrow at eight,' and he planted a swift kiss on the top of her head.

CHAPTER FOUR

WILLOW lay on her back in the king-sized bed and longed for sleep. It had been an hour since she had left Theo's suite, embarrassed and, if she was honest, burning with frustration. She was still burning; she could still feel the touch of his mouth on hers, could still taste him on her tongue and could still feel the need clawing in her belly. No other man had ever made her feel like this. She had only ever dated a couple of people during the past few years. The latest was a perfectly pleasant man called Dave, who was a GP. They were close but their relationship had not even progressed past a kiss. So why, oh, why was she such a pushover for a man like Theo?

It was so unfair and so unexpected, moisture glazed her eyes. What should have been one of the most triumphant days of her life had ended in disaster, and a solitary tear flowed down her cheek. Until yesterday she would have sworn Theo Kadros meant less than nothing to her. For the past nine years she had lived with the conviction he was beneath contempt. She still thought that, but somehow after meeting Theo again today, talking to him, it was making her question her own behaviour.

A deep sigh escaped her... If he ever found out she had given birth to his child, his son, and never told him...she didn't dare think what he might do to her. Yet it had seemed the right thing to do, the only thing to do at the time.

Closing her eyes, she let the memories flood back of her

arrival in India and the last few precious months she had spent with her mother.

It had never really entered her head that she might be pregnant because Theo had used condoms. She had thought that his mention at the airport of the possibility she might become pregnant had just been a ruse to keep in touch. She had been furious with him, and ashamed of herself, and still young enough to see everything in black and white with no grey area in between. In her mind he was a womanising swine that would quite happily take any girl to bed. His suggestion they spend the weekend together had simply been a ploy to send her back to her own room. She had convinced herself he probably had girlfriends dotted all around the world that his poor innocent fiancée knew nothing about, and he had simply wanted to add Willow to his list.

She had been accepted at Oxford to read English in September, and she'd been determined to put Theo Kadros out of her mind, and enjoy her holiday in India with her mother. She had realised she had made a disastrous mistake succumbing to the sexual overtures of a sophisticated, experienced man, and had mistaken lust for love. She had put it down to experience; determined to learn by it and get over it.

But as the long summer had progressed her mother had become more and more worried about her. Willow had honestly thought her lack of energy and occasional sickness had been because of the hot climate, and her bruised heart. It had only been after nine weeks when her mother had taken her to a doctor, that she'd discovered she was pregnant.

It had been her mother who had convinced her to return to England and make the arrangements to postpone her university entrance for a year and insisted she contact the father straight away.

Willow had reluctantly agreed. She had told her mother her ex-boyfriend was the brother of a friend, implying she had known him for some time. She had been too ashamed to tell her mother it had just been a one-night stand. She had returned to London, and had called at Theo's house in Mayfair prepared to tell him she was pregnant.

But it had not worked out like that. Oh, Willow had gone to the house all right! But only to find it covered in scaffolding. The contractor, British Land Ltd, had been turning it into prestigious offices, and the foreman had told her he had no idea where the last residents had gone.

Tired and frightened, Willow had returned to her family home in Devon. She had called her mother, and told her the ex-boyfriend was out of the country at the moment. Her mother had told Willow not to worry, her tour of duty in India would be finished in ten days, and when she got back they could contact the boy together.

But her mother had never returned to England and Willow had never seen her again.

Willow rolled over on her stomach and buried her head in the pillow. After all these years, it still brought a tear to her eyes when she thought of her mother. It had been such a needless way to die. She had been on her way back from work at the British Embassy to the apartment she'd rented in the city, when she had been caught up in a riot. The Indian army had fired over the heads of the rioters, but by horrible chance a bullet had ricocheted off a building and hit her beloved mother. She had died instantly.

The Foreign Office had been very helpful, but to the pregnant Willow, who had lost her mother and grandmother within six months of each other, it had been devastating. She had numbly agreed to everything that had been suggested, and she could still remember with horror a dark-suited man arriving at the cottage and presenting her with a brass urn containing her mother's ashes.

For months she'd been swamped in grief and it had only been with the help of her grandmother's neighbour, Tess, that Willow had managed to carry on. At seven months pregnant Willow had finally come out of her haze of grief and concentrated on the child growing inside her. She'd decided it was time to do as her mother had wanted, and tell the father. Only it had been too late…

Sitting on the train to London, with the address of Theo Kadros's British office in her pocket, Willow had opened the magazine she had bought to read on the journey. There in front of her she had seen the marriage of Theo Kadros to Dianne displayed in a dozen glossy pictures of the happy couple. She had left the train at the next stop and gone straight back home.

Swinging her legs over the side of the bed, Willow sat up and brushed the moisture from her eyes with the back of her hand. She was never going to sleep, and she refused to indulge in any more grief or self-pity. Her mind had been made up for her years ago, and she was determined to stick by her original decision. It was too late to change now…

So by the same token the last thing she needed was to meet Theo Kadros for breakfast or at any other time, for that matter.

A quick glance at her wrist-watch told her it was two-thirty in the morning; no chance of a train back to Devon tonight. What the hell? She was a published author who had just signed a lucrative deal for film rights; she could afford it this once, and it was an emergency…

Quickly and quietly she washed and dressed in blue jeans and a checked shirt and slipped a blue lambswool sweater over the top. She packed her overnight case and glanced around the room. Spying the list of pamphlets on the table, she quickly flicked through them until she found what she wanted. She dialled the number and breathed a sigh of relief. A car would be waiting for her in ten minutes.

It didn't matter about the hotel bill, as it was in the name of her publishers and they were paying.

She did not use the lift, but walked down the stairs from her third-floor room. She had noted that the staircase ended very close to the exit door, and would save her having to cross the foyer, where somebody might see her.

'Madam, do you need a cab?' the doorman asked, blinking; the poor man was half asleep.

'No, I have a car picking me up,' she said truthfully, and slipped him the key to her room and a high denomination note, and suddenly he was wide-awake. He opened the hotel door for her, and escorted her to the pavement without batting an eyelid!

Willow heaved a sigh of relief as she slid into the back seat of the waiting car. 'You know the way?'

A cheerful female face turned back to smile at her. 'Yes, ma'am. I checked on the way over here; this is the best fare I have had in months.'

On that note, Willow finally closed her eyes. The immense relief she felt at having slipped away from the hotel and Theo, combined with the steady drone of the car's engine, encouraged her to sleep. Within minutes she had dozed off into a restless slumber.

Damn it to hell! Theo swore as he drained the bottle of whisky into the crystal glass. The witch had turned him inside out all over again, but this time…this time he had decided to proceed with caution where the lovely Willow was concerned.

It had nearly killed him to let her walk out of his suite, hence the almost half a bottle of whisky he had downed since she'd left. He didn't usually drink much at all. He had learnt his lesson the hard way.

After Willow had left him standing at the airport, feeling furious and betrayed, he had vowed to banish her from his mind. The method he'd chosen was to drink too much, which had resulted in him making a foolish decision. He had got back together with Dianne, and agreed to marry her. She was a great lawyer but not a great wife, and their marriage had very quickly sobered him up. When he had found his wife in bed with another man, divorce had been inevitable, and he wasn't sorry.

Contrary to the opinion of the popular press, he was not the playboy they painted him. He had had three mistresses in the four years since his divorce. The latest one being Christine, who lived in Athens. Recently he had contemplated marrying her simply as a means to provide him with an heir. His work was his life. A life he had been quite content with until he had stood in the hotel reception this morning and watched Willow Blain walk down the stairs.

Draining the glass, he strolled over to the telephone and gave the night-duty receptionist his instructions. He wanted a wake-up call at six-thirty. But more importantly if Miss Blain tried to book out, he was to be informed immediately. His mind was made up; Willow would not escape him so easily this time.

At eight the next morning a snarling Theo spun the hotel register around and read the entry. 'Willow Blain. Care of Henkon Publishing' and the address.

'What time did she leave?' he demanded icily of the cowering manager.

'According to the night porter, about three in the morning. A car was waiting for her, apparently.'

Famed for his business acumen and his quick, incisive mind, Theo was in danger of losing it completely and sacking everyone on the spot. Until it struck him there was something very odd about Willow's behaviour. He wasn't a fool. He knew women, and he knew the sexual tension, the chemistry between them was electric. He could, with very little persuasion, have had Willow in his bed last night.

Willow might not want to renew their relationship, but all she had to do was say, 'No'. So why did she feel the need to escape in the middle of the night? That was the real question. He had to give Willow credit—she was crafty. A wry smile twisted his firm mouth. The woman wrote detective novels; he should have expected as much. But the lovely Willow obviously had something to hide, and Theo was not going to rest until he found out.

It was eight in the morning when the cab pulled up outside Willow's thatched cottage overlooking the river. Willow paid the driver and, with a sigh of relief, let herself into her home. Stephen was staying with Tess and her husband at their home a hundred yards further up the road, and they were not expecting her back until this afternoon.

She glanced around the familiar hall and smiled. She had probably overreacted, leaving London in the middle of the night, but she didn't care. She was home, and it felt great. Running upstairs to her bedroom, she placed her weekend case on the bed and swiftly unpacked. She took a quick shower and washed her hair. Standing in front of the mirror, she set about drying her hair. As she glanced at the naked reflection of herself a vivid mental image of Theo's dark head lowered over her breasts, his sensuous mouth suckling the rose-tipped peaks, suddenly flashed in her mind. A shaft of heat lanced through her slender body and she almost groaned. No! her mind cried. Sex and all that was behind her, had been for nine years, and that was the way it was going to stay. She continued drying her hair with more force than was necessary.

Returning to the bedroom, she looked out of the window at the view of the river sparkling in the bright early morning sunshine and smiled again. This was her life now and it was a good one. So what if she didn't have a man in her life? She didn't need one. Stephen was more than enough for her.

She quickly put on clean briefs and a multi-coloured Indian cotton summer dress with short sleeves, the skirt swinging around her calves. She slipped her feet into flat sandals, and with a flick of her long hair she went back downstairs.

She'd have a quick breakfast and then call at Tess's and surprise Stephen. Then she would walk him to school as she usually did. Everything back to normal and no more city jaunts for her, she vowed. It was the first time since Stephen was born that she had spent a night away from him, and she had no intention of repeating the exercise.

Ten minutes later as she opened the gate to Tess's cottage the front door opened, and her heart expanded in her breast at the sight of the dark-haired dynamo of a boy that shot out.

'Mum... Mum, you're back. I have had a really great time, you wouldn't believe,' Stephen called out as he ran full tilt down the garden path followed by a beaming Tess. 'The reporter from the local paper called and interviewed me, and he took a photograph of me. He said my picture might be in the paper, and that you were going to make tons of money.'

Shock held her rigid for an instant. 'That's great,' she finally managed to say, and swept the firm young body of her son up in her arms, and hugged him so tightly he yelped.

'Hey, Mum, put me down. I'm eight, not a baby.' Reluctantly she let him go.

'I didn't think you would mind,' her friend Tess said, grinning. 'You winning the award is the most excitement this village has ever seen.'

'Thanks,' Willow said, trying to smile. Inside she was horrified at the thought of Stephen's photo appearing in a newspaper. But Tess did not seem to notice anything was amiss and continued speaking.

'How did you get back so quick?'

'Well…'

'No, it doesn't matter. I guess you want to walk Stephen to school. Call in on your way back. I will have the coffee ready and I want to hear every little detail.'

Stephen continued chattering nineteen to the dozen as they headed for the primary school two hundred yards away and for the first time in his young life Willow was barely listening to what he was saying, feelings of fright and panic already consuming her. She tried to tell herself it was a local paper, very few people read it, and she was worrying for nothing, but mixed in with her fear was guilt.

She glanced down at her son's beaming, excited face and wondered if she had made the right decision all those years ago. Stephen had not looked particularly like Theo when he was born. His eyes had been a deep blue, but within months they had turned dark brown. Most of the people in the village, because of his black curly hair, had automatically said he looked like Willow. But as he had grown older the baby curls had some how straightened out, and his skin tone had become much darker than hers. More and more Willow could see his father in his features.

'Anyway,' Stephen said, 'when the man asked who my father was, Tess told him to stop, and then he left.'

'What?' Willow exclaimed, the mention of *father* registering like a bullet to the brain. 'Well, that was very wise of Tess.' She smiled down into his suddenly serious face, and felt even worse.

'Mum, you know you said my father married someone else and then vanished to the other side of the world but you didn't know where? Well, now you are going to make a lot of money, do you think we could look for him? Today is the last day at school, and next week is half-term holiday, so we could start looking from tomorrow.' He looked at her with such innocent, trusting eyes her heart turned over in her breast.

'Well, I don't see why not,' she conceded, and then felt terrible for lying to him. But was it a lie? She had always known deep in her heart that at some point Stephen would want to meet his dad, and the event of the last twenty-four hours had simply reinforced her belief.

Smiling down at Stephen, she added, 'In any case, a holiday will do us both good.' The idea of taking Stephen away somewhere for a week suddenly seemed a brilliant idea. By the time they returned the press would have hopefully forgotten all about them. Part of her problem solved for the moment, she was relieved to see Stephen's friend Tommy run towards him as they approached the schoolyard, Stephen's thoughts of his father evaporating as he eagerly joined in his friend and vanished into the school building, without a backward glance.

'Well,' Tess exclaimed, 'tell all! Is the gorgeous Mr Carlavitch as handsome and sexy in the flesh? And is he going to make you rich? And, most important, did you fancy him?'

Sitting at Tess's kitchen table nursing a cup of coffee,

Willow laughed. It was either that or cry. 'I don't know,' she responded honestly. 'He was quite attractive I suppose.' She had had another man entirely on her mind during that time, and still had.

'Are you all right?' Tess frowned. 'I thought you would be ecstatic winning the award and everything, yet you look a bit done in.'

'Yes, I am a bit,' Willow said, getting to her feet, grateful for the excuse to get away and be alone with her turbulent thoughts. 'I did travel half the night in a car, you know. Thanks a million for looking after Stephen, I really appreciate it. I think I will just nip into the village for some milk, and then go home to rest for a while.'

'Of course. I don't know what I was thinking of. I'll catch you later.'

'I'll pop back in after I collect Stephen from school this afternoon. Actually, I am thinking of taking him away tomorrow for the half-term holiday, down to Falmouth like we did last year, and a trip to France for a day or so. He likes the boat trip and he deserves a treat; he has been so good.'

'Good idea. But in that case you will need all the sleep you can get.' Tess chuckled.

But when Willow returned to her cottage thirty minutes later sleep was the last thing on her mind. After she'd accepted the congratulations of what appeared to be half the village, clustered around the post office, someone had complimented Willow on the picture in one of the national tabloids. In horror she had scanned the photo. It was her, all right, standing in the foyer of the hotel the day before. But alongside the picture of her was another one of Stephen, obviously thanks to the miracle of a computer and modern technology. When she read the article she felt sick.

Willow moved around her much-loved home, scrubbing

and cleaning in a frenzy of activity, anything to take her mind off her troubles. She paused for a long moment in Stephen's bedroom, a sad smile curving her lush mouth. The Thomas the Tank Engine wallpaper he had loved when a toddler had been replaced by cool blue paper, posters of his favourite cars adorned the walls, and a computer stood on his desk. At eight he was clearly growing up, and she had buried her head in the sand for far too long. His demand today that they go and look for his dad had proved that.

Fearful for the future and what it held, she gave up any idea of lying down to rest, and walked back downstairs. She had a horrible premonition that Stephen might get his wish a lot sooner than he expected. She knew Theo Kadros was still in London. She tried to tell herself she had nothing to worry about—a man like Theo only read the financial papers. But she could not shrug off the fear that somehow he was going to discover her secret.

A stony-faced Theo glanced through the *Financial Times* waiting for the car that was to take him to his meeting, but his mind was not on business. He had called Henkon Publishing and asked for Willow's address and been turned down flat.

'Sir.'

'Yes,' he snapped at the hotel manager.

'I know this is not the kind of newspaper you usually read, but I thought you might be interested.' He wasn't the manager of a top-class hotel without having a good brain and good insight where people were concerned. He had a shrewd idea that Mr Kadros might be very interested and hopefully very appreciative of his suggestion. 'It is a very good picture. Don't you think?' He handed the paper to his boss folded at the correct page.

Theo glanced at the picture, and then at the smaller one next to it, and looked again. His dark eyes widened incredulously, and then blazed black with fury. His lips tightened into a hard, bitter line creating a ring of white around his mouth as he read the accompanying article.

Who would have guessed that the winner of this year's Crime Writers' Prize, J. W. Paxton, for his novel A Class Act Murder, *would turn out to be not a man but a woman? The stunningly attractive Willow Blain, and yes, folks, that is her real name.*

The film rights were sold only hours after the award ceremony to Mr Carlavitch, the famous American film producer.

Willow is also a single mother, but without a marriage behind her, living in Devon with an eight-year-old son she has brought up entirely on her own.

Theo took out his mobile phone, barked out a few instructions, then dialled again and cancelled his arrangements for the day.

CHAPTER FIVE

WITH a hotel booked in Falmouth for tomorrow night, and
their suitcases packed, Willow was ready to leave first thing
in the morning. A week away together would do them both
good, she told herself. As for looking for Stephen's father…
She couldn't lie to her son, but at least the break would
give her time to come to terms with the fact that Stephen
had a right to know who his father was and maybe some
time in the future meet him. But not yet…

Meeting Theo for a drink last night had been a huge
mistake and had seriously dented her pride and her confi-
dence. Convinced she could handle the situation with mature sophistication, she had been terribly shocked to realise
that, in the sexual stakes, she was no further forward where
Theo was concerned than when she was an eighteen-year-
old virgin. She hadn't been able to resist him then, and it
had been humiliating to realise that nothing much had
changed.

True she had said, 'No,' and escaped, but not before
she'd been forced to face the shattering realisation that for
some bizarre reason her body seemed to be programmed to
respond instantly and helplessly to one particular man:
Theo Kadros. It was only lust. An unfortunate chemical
reaction, nothing more. She knew this, but even so she
needed time to build up her defences before even contem-
plating telling him he had a son.

Still too ill at ease to rest in the now spotless house, she
walked out into the garden. Perhaps a stroll along the riv-
erbank would ease the emotional turmoil the events of the

past twenty-four hours had created in her mind. Spying a thistle among the profusion of flowers that lined the path, she stooped and tugged viciously at the offending weed. The spikes pierced the palm of her hand, and she cursed long and bitterly under her breath. The brief physical pain was nothing compared to how foolish she felt. She had allowed her editor, Louise, to persuade her into entering her book for the award, and to attend the ceremony in London.

She had succumbed to flattery and paid the price for it. Hadn't her grandmother always said, 'Get too big for you boots, and the chances are you will end up without any'? If she had thought the thing through logically she would never have taken the risk of exposing herself to the press, and especially not Stephen...

Willow straightened up as she heard the sound of a car approaching. A big black Mercedes almost filled the narrow road. Surprised, she watched as the car drew level with her garden. A car door slammed and the figure of a tall dark man appeared. He stared at her across the roof of the car, and the blood froze in her veins. He must have seen the newspaper, and put two and two together.

Theo's hard black eyes swept over Willow from head to toe. He noticed her exquisite face framed by the silken mass of black hair tumbling over her shoulders; the long cotton dress skimming her slender figure, baring her arms, and just the merest hint of firm white breasts, and, lower, a glimpse of leg and ankles. He wanted to kill her.

Once he had taken her innocence and felt thoroughly ashamed of himself when he had discovered how young she was. Anger, regret and guilt had plagued him, and almost unmanned him. In consequence he had resumed a sexual relationship with Dianne, and had hastily leapt into a marriage that had never been going to last. The reason being the image of Willow's exquisite body, wildly responsive in his arms, was etched into his brain for all time.

For years he had still ached to possess this one woman again; hers was the face that haunted his waking and sleeping dreams.

Only yesterday he had thought the gods were smiling on him and had given him a second chance. A harsh, cynical smile twisted his wide, sensual mouth. Not any more... She was no innocent deserving sympathy, never had been... She was a secretive, conniving bitch, and she had committed the most heinous crime against him and his family it was possible to envisage, and he had every intention of making her pay.

'The original earth mother—how charming,' he mockingly opined, strolling around the bonnet of the car.

Standing frozen to the spot, Willow couldn't believe her eyes. It was Theo Kadros, but it was impossible. It was a five-hour drive from London. That was in the middle of the night with no traffic on the roads. There was no way he could have made the journey this morning. His tall, broad-shouldered frame was immaculately clad in a dark blue pinstriped business suit. A pale blue silk shirt emphasised his bronzed features and was complemented by a finely striped tie.

'What, nothing to say, Willow?' She simply stared at him, her heart pounding in her chest as he opened the garden gate and in a few lithe strides stopped inches from her.

'Cat got your tongue, Willow?' His black eyes, as cold as ice, stared down into hers.

'Hello, Theo, nice to see you again.' She made a polite response, too shocked to do anything else, and looked bemusedly past him to the car. 'How did you get here?'

'Let's be civil, by all means,' Theo drawled scathingly. 'My private jet was waiting at London City airport. I was supposed to attend a meeting this morning and then fly out to Greece this evening; instead I had my pilot fly me to Exeter airport, and arranged for a car to be waiting. It is barely an hour's drive to here.'

'Oh, I see.' And in that moment she saw a lot more than she wanted too. Theo, his great body taut, was watching her with a hard, challenging gleam in his dark eyes, and her heart sank like a stone. Did she really have the strength to protect her son from this man, to fight him? A man of his wealth and power. A man who could hop in his jet and appear on her doorstep at the drop of a hat. But, more, did she have the right? She was no longer sure.

'Hi, Willow. Congratulations on the award.' A voice floated over the garden gate. Willow looked nervously over Theo's shoulder, and then smiled at Tess's husband cycling past on his way home.

'Thanks, Bob.' And she waved.

'Damn it to hell!' Theo suddenly exploded, and, grabbing her arm in an iron grip, he dragged her towards the open front door and shoved her into the hall, slamming the door behind him. 'You can cut out the country-girl routine in front of me, Willow. You are the most devious bloody woman I have ever met,' he snarled. 'My God! Why didn't you tell me I had a son?'

'How did you find me?' she shot back. She knew her publisher would never reveal her address. Willow realised that if Theo got the idea she was hiding something it would simply confirm his suspicions. Not waiting for an answer, she added, 'And anyway, what makes you think my child has anything to do with you?' she demanded in a cool, polite voice. Inside she was shaking like a leaf.

'Don't bother to deny it,' he said harshly, his fingers tightening on her arm. 'I saw the photograph in the newspaper. I had my people check the boy's birth date at the register office, and, surprise, surprise, he was born at home, at this address. It was not terribly difficult to discover, Willow.'

'No. Oh, no,' she murmured. Her worst fear had been realised. Bowing her head to evade his searing gaze, she knew with a despairing sense of inevitability that her world would never be the same again.

'You dare to deny it?' he declared contemptuously, completely misreading her negative response. 'Then I will see you in court, and show you up for the little liar you are. By the time my lawyers are finished with you, *you* will be begging *me* to see our son. Believe me, Willow, I can and I will do it.' The cold menace in his voice sent shivers of fear down her spine. 'You have deprived me of my child for eight years.' Grasping her chin with his free hand, he tilted her face up to his.

'Hanging your head in shame now? It is a bit late for that, Willow,' he opined scathingly, forcing her to look at him. 'Because it was not only me you deprived of the child.' The hard bones of his jaw and chin tightened with suppressed emotion. 'The one thing my father wanted before he died was to see me with a family of my own. He died three years ago, and went to his grave never knowing he had a grandson, all because of you.' The bitterness in the black eyes that held hers chilled her to the bone. 'No more lies, Willow. Where is my son? I want to see him now!'

'He is at school until three-thirty.' She told the truth; there was no point trying to deny it. 'And I'm sorry about your...' She was about to finish, but as she looked into his bitter, hate-filled eyes the words of conventional sympathy stuck in her throat. When Stephen was born, it had never entered her head that, by not informing the father, at the same time she might be depriving a decent old man of a much-longed-for grandson.

'Oh, you are going to be sorry. I can promise you that.' Theo tightened his grip and she winced.

'You're hurting me,' she snapped, the physical pain cutting through her mental anguish and restoring some of her usual spirit. She refused to feel guilty about Theo's father. If Theo himself had not been a two-timing swine of a man and already married when Stephen had been born things might have worked out differently. If anyone was to blame it was Theo, she thought scathingly, and his hedonistic lifestyle.

'You don't know what pain is…yet.' He smiled a cold, humourless smile, but did release her and glanced around the small wood-panelled hall.

Theo had to look away from her because for the first time in his life he felt dangerously close to inflicting violence on a woman. He battled to contain his rage and noted a door on either side of the hall. Both doors were partially opened, one revealing the living room, and the other a dining-room-cum-study. A third door at the rear led to the kitchen, and a narrow steep staircase led to the upper floor. 'I might have guessed,' Theo drawled with a negative shake of his dark head. It was like stepping back in time, the perfect hideaway. Her friends had not been far wrong when they had nicknamed her The Mole.

Guessed what? Willow wondered, but said nothing. She continued to watch him with wary eyes, and began nervously rubbing her bare arm where his fingers had left their mark. Theo's tall, broad figure seemed to fill the small hall, making her feel positively claustrophobic in her own home. She frantically racked her brain for some way to get rid of him.

His temper now back under control, Theo cast her a cynical glance. 'I will wait in here, and, as you did not turn up for our breakfast together,' he said with biting sarcasm, 'you can make me lunch.' With this, he strolled through the open living-room door.

Make him lunch! He was in her house for less than two minutes and already he was ordering her around. The cool cheek of the man. Willow silently fumed but followed behind him, knowing exactly what he was going to encounter next. She decided that she was not going to warn him... Let him knock himself out, the arrogant devil.

Low oak beams crossed the plastered ceiling. The room was furnished with all her grandmother's old oak furniture, and knick-knacks and it hadn't changed much since she was a child. She had modernised some rooms, but essentially the style was seventeenth century, in keeping with the house.

As she walked through the door she watched as Theo turned around in the middle of the room, and deftly dipped his head, narrowly missing one of the low beams. Trust him to duck in time, she thought bitterly, but then by all accounts he'd spent his whole life ducking and diving in the business world, which was why he was so filthy rich. She eyed him balefully. He had never looked more foreign, more Greek to her than he did right now, and she wondered how on earth she was going to come to some agreement with him over Stephen.

'You certainly fit your nickname—The Mole.' Theo raised one black sardonic eyebrow. 'Buried away in an ancient dark-beamed house, overlooking the river in a tiny village that does not even appear on a map, blindly keeping yourself and my son hidden from sight.'

She allowed no one to attack her home, or her lifestyle, and certainly not a jet-setting, womanising multimillionaire with more money than sense. She had seen in magazines the huge villa Theo had built for his wife, Dianne, and hadn't been impressed.

'I like it,' she snapped back, 'and so does Stephen. It is *our* home, and we have lots of friends and are very happy here.'

But his sarcastic comment had hit a nerve; she had always been a secret, sensitive person, and very much a creature of habit. When she had lost both her grandmother and mother in a few short months, almost everyone in the village had rallied around the pregnant eighteen-year-old. This house, which she had known all her life, had become her sanctuary; she loved the place. Free of a mortgage and with her mother's life insurance policy, and the income she received from her writing, she had been able to stay here with her son, safe and secure among friends.

She had given up any thought of going to university, not willing to move across the country and live among strangers. She also hated the idea of putting her baby into a crèche when she could stop where she was and look after him herself. But she also knew that she did tend to ignore anything that might upset her cosy lifestyle.

Realistically she had known for some time that Stephen wanted to meet his father. He had dropped plenty of hints, and she'd known she was going to have to do something about it. Maybe subconsciously she had allowed her editor to talk her into going to London and revealing her true identity as a first step towards facing up to her wider responsibility and seeking out Theo Kadros.

Even so, she sure as hell had not expected him to turn up on her doorstep today and start making derogatory comments about her house. She could feel her anger increasing by the minute.

'You were not invited to my home, Theo, and I don't do lunches. So please, feel free to leave.' She stared defiantly up at him, the atmosphere between them crackling with tension.

'No, you are not getting rid of me so easily this time, Willow,' Theo responded, casually lowering his long length down onto the leather sofa. He glanced up into her furious blue eyes, his own a bland, unemotional black. 'I am staying here until I get my son.'

Not until he *saw* his son, she noted, but until he *got* his son, a statement of fact issued with all the cool assurance of a man who always got what he wanted. She doubted if the person was born who could get one over the mighty Theo Kadros. The fact that she had managed to do so for eight years was a miracle in itself. But in the face of his calm assumption that he would get his son her fears for the future were increased a thousandfold.

'He is not your son,' she began, her blue eyes flashing defiance. 'He—'

'You little bitch,' he cut in, leaping to his feet, and in one swift movement he grasped a clump of her hair and twisted the thick silken strands around his wrist and tugged her head back. His other arm latched around her waist and hauled her hard against him.

'You still dare to deny it. You dare to play games with me even now,' he grated, his self-control completely deserting him. She saw the glitter of violent fury in his black eyes, and for a moment her heart quaked with fear.

But she refused to be intimidated. Stephen was *her* son; and she was prepared to fight for him. She knew instinctively that she could not afford to appear weak in front of Theo Kadros.

'Get your hands off me, you b—' she gasped, but was prevented from saying any more by a second cruel tug on her hair.

'I'd like to strangle you,' he snarled, 'but you aren't

worth swinging for.' And his mouth crashed down on hers with a cruel force that drove the breath from her body.

She was crushed against him so closely she was aware of every bone in his huge body. She only had a brief fleeting glimpse of the merciless intent in his dark eyes before his mouth hardened and he forced her lips apart and began a ruthless exploration of the moist interior of her mouth. It was a savage and hungry passion that had nothing to do with love and everything to do with a primitive male desire to punish and dominate.

She tried to resist but his hand curved around the back of her head, and held her immobile while he continued to plunder her mouth. He eased the pressure a little to allow her to breathe and a slight moan escaped her. Then the hand at her waist was holding her crushed against his lower body, slid over the curve of her buttocks and made her instantly aware of his fiercely aroused state. At the same time the punishing pressure of his mouth subtly altered, and, to her horror, a treacherous heat ignited deep down inside her.

She closed her eyes tightly; it should not be like this, her mind cried. Shaken as she was by the destructive power of his passion she was still capable of realising that he was using his superior sexual expertise as a weapon to deliberately humiliate her. But with the ever-softening sensuality of Theo's lips and tongue and his hand moving up her body to her breast, the fine cotton of her dress no barrier as deftly the first few buttons flew open, Willow knew she was in imminent danger of falling under his spell all over again.

She wasn't wearing a bra and his hand cupped her naked breast, his thumb sliding over the tender peak, and she was helpless to prevent her body responding. She groaned a low, soft sound of both desire and despair intermingled, and involuntarily her slender arms linked around his neck.

She then surrendered to the heat, the hunger and the fierce wave of passion suddenly sweeping through her body.

Theo slowly raised his dark head. 'That's better, Willow,' he said roughly. His long fingers were still covering her breasts, deliberately moving from one to the other, playing with the aching, rigid peaks. She opened her eyes, and gazed up into his darkly attractive face, hot and breathless with sensual excitement.

He was staring down at her, unable to hide the desire in his eyes, his breathing as erratic as hers, a muscle beating in his jaw. But his voice was remarkably steady as he added, 'Now I know coming to an arrangement will not be a problem.' She caught the gleam of cynical triumph in his smouldering eyes and it was like a douche of cold water.

What on earth was she doing? She must be mad. This man wanted her son, and for the second time in less than twenty-four hours she was lying in his arms, her dress half off, gazing at him like a besotted fool. Terrified by her own emotional frailty, she wrenched herself from his arms and darted out of the room. She ran into the kitchen, fumbling with the buttons of her dress, her legs trembling and almost collapsing with shame and embarrassment.

Leaning over the sink, she turned on the cold-water tap and splashed her face with water in a desperate attempt to cool her overheated flesh. Straightening, she picked up the hand towel from the rail and dried her face. Coffee, thick and black, that was what she needed. She realised it had been a long night and an even more harrowing morning and she needed to start thinking sensibly and quickly. She filled the kettle and reached for the jar of coffee in the cupboard with a hand that shook.

'Ah, there you are.' Spinning around, she almost dropped the coffee jar as Theo, her nemesis, walked in.

Willow glared at him. He'd removed his tie, and the

open-necked shirt only served to draw her attention to his strong, tanned throat. She gulped and felt hot colour return to her cheeks as she recalled how only minutes ago her arms had been wrapped intimately around that throat. It was so unfair—he looked even more incredibly attractive than ever, and he was in total control, she thought bitterly.

'Coffee. Good, I could do with a cup, and I hope your hasty exit means you are going to make me lunch. I am starving,' Theo drawled smoothly, and, as cool as a cucumber, pulled out one of the four pine chairs that surrounded the square breakfast table and sat down. 'We can talk just as easily in here.'

She didn't trust herself to speak, and simply stared at him as his dark, curious gaze swept around the room, lingering on the window that opened out onto the back garden and the fields beyond.

'One thing I will say for this little house, it does have rather good views.' Theo turned his dark head towards her, his eyes taking in her beautiful face still tinged scarlet with embarrassment. His gaze flickered over her slender figure before lingering on the bodice of her dress, where in her haste she had fastened the buttons in the wrong buttonholes, and the curve of one breast was exposed to reveal the dark aureole surrounding a small, tight nipple. 'Both outside and in,' he added.

As a gentleman he should tell her, but after what she had done to him he had no inclination to act the gentleman. Let her find out for herself, and in the meantime he could sit back and enjoy the view. He glanced up into her wary eyes, a broad smile slashing across his handsome face, his dark eyes lit with amusement.

His grin was so open that for a moment Willow was tempted to respond, but, tearing her gaze away, she muttered, 'Flattery will get you nowhere,' and she turned back to the bench. Reaching up for two cups, she plonked them down on the worktop. 'But I will make you a coffee.' At least that way she could keep her back to him for a while. 'There is a good pub and restaurant a few miles back the way you came that serves a very nice lunch, if you are really hungry.' With a bit of luck he would take himself off to the pub and, with a bit of breathing space, she might just possibly get her chaotic thoughts into some kind of order before she had to pick up Stephen.

'You don't really imagine for a minute that I am going to leave you alone,' he prompted, moving across the room to lean casually against the bench beside her. 'And surely you cannot be so cruel as to refuse to feed a starving man? Because of you, Willow, I ate very little breakfast.'

She ignored his barbed reminder and cast him a sidelong glance. 'You don't look like any starving man I have ever seen. But, if you insist, I think I have some eggs and home-made bread rolls.' Slowly it was beginning to dawn on Willow that there was no point in fighting Theo. She needed to keep her temper, and her arguments, for the big issue: Stephen.

Ten minutes later she placed a plate containing a cheese omelette and salad on the table in front of Theo, accompanied by the butter dish and a basket of crusty bread rolls.

Willow did not want to eat, in fact she felt sick, but Theo had insisted she join him. His earlier anger appeared to have vanished and she agreed, hoping to keep him sweet. As she watched Theo wolf down his food with apparent enjoyment she pushed hers around the plate, pretending to eat, her stomach curled in knots of nervous tension.

'That was excellent, Willow. I must say you surprised me. The omelette was perfect and the bread rolls were a work of art; you are a wonderful cook.' Theo grinned, leaning back in his chair. 'I don't think I have ever had a girlfriend who made her own bread,' he offered, amusement in his tone.

Rising to her feet, she collected the plates and glanced down at him. 'You still haven't,' she responded bluntly. 'Your type of girlfriends are well-documented fashion plates who probably don't have the time between visiting the beautician's and the hairdresser, and of course pandering to your every whim, to do anything else,' she ended dryly. Turning, she crossed to the dishwasher and loaded the plates, and then plugged in the kettle. 'More coffee?' she asked without looking around. Theo disturbed her on so many levels she was having trouble concentrating.

'Yes.' She nearly jumped out of her skin as the affirmative was murmured very close to her ear. She had not heard his silent approach, and he was now standing right behind her. 'But I think you are going to need the coffee more before this day is out, because you are quite wrong, Willow.'

No humour now. Willow heard the threat in his voice, and she straightened up, her shoulders tense, but she was incapable of turning around as his warm breath brushed against her cheek.

'True, you are no longer my girlfriend—that was a short-lived but very productive episode, as I have just discovered. But, make no mistake, I am no longer the poor fool who was put off by your lie about the morning-after pill,' he drawled silkily. 'This time I don't just want you as a girl-friend. This time I'll marry you if I have to, but I do want my son.'

'What?' She spun around. 'Have you taken leave of your senses? I wouldn't marry you if you were the last man on earth!' she exclaimed, horrified at his suggestion.

Theo stared down at her for a long moment, taking in the stunned expression in her dazzling blue eyes. He then gave a slight shrug of his broad shoulders. 'Tough.' He paused, one dark brow arching sardonically, 'But it is not your choice, Willow. It is mine.'

'You can't say that,' she cried, agitation making her voice rise. 'It's ridiculous. Marriage is a diabolical suggestion.'

He gave a scornful laugh. 'Nowhere near as diabolical as you depriving me of my son for eight years. I had to learn of his existence, even his name, from a cheap tabloid. Well, you are not getting the chance to humiliate me, or lie to me, again. If we marry our son will have both parents. It is the simplest solution and the only thing we need to discuss is what you have told Stephen about his absent father.' He stared down at her, ferocious tension written into every hard line of his strong face as he added in a voice devoid of all emotion, 'And if you made the mistake of telling him I was dead, I might very well kill you myself.'

The threat was there in his eyes and in the powerful body towering over her. Suddenly something seemed to snap in Willow's brain, and without thinking she lashed out at him, her hand connecting hard on his lean cheek. 'Don't you dare threaten me, you no-good womanising bastard. No one ever deprived you of anything in your life, and you have the nerve to threaten me and my son.'

Theo stared down at her, his eyes cold as ice. 'That was a very stupid thing to do, Willow. I want my son, but I don't *have* to take you. My offer of marriage was one of kindness, but a court order will do just as well,' he drawled cynically.

'As if I care about your kindness. You deserved it,' she snapped, almost choking with anger. 'No court in the land would give you custody, you arrogant devil, not when I tell them the truth.'

'And the truth, as we both know,' he sneered, grasping her by the shoulders, 'is that you were a precocious young girl who wanted nothing more than to get rid of her virginity. So desperate, in fact, that you slept with some unsuspecting male. Then you quite deliberately denied that you could possibly be pregnant, and quite deliberately deprived the father of his son.'

'My God, that is rich coming from you,' she cried. 'You took one look at me and seduced me into your bed, in your own house, where your sister and her friends were supposed to be looking after me, conveniently forgetting you were engaged to be married at the time!' She tried to twist free from his hold but he slammed her back against the bench.

'Don't try to lie your way out of it, Willow. I was not engaged to anyone.'

'Oh, please, save me!' Willow mocked. 'I answered the telephone call from your fiancée myself, Theo. She wasn't surprised you were still asleep, because she had apparently kept you up in her bed all night the previous evening.'

Theo's hands slackened on her shoulders, and he stared down into her wild blue eyes. She obviously believed what she was saying. Then he remembered the conversation he had had with Anna that fateful morning, nine years ago. Willow had taken the first of many calls from Dianne. He had to admit Willow was right, he had been up all night, but as for the rest... His dark brows drew together in a deep, puzzled frown.

But Willow was past noticing, she was on a roll. All the pain and hurt she had buried deep for nine years came bursting out. 'The woman you married six months later, Theo, before Stephen was even born. You do remember her, don't you? You rotten, two-timing, lousy bastard. And yet you have the colossal nerve to stand there and try to blame me.' She shook her head, her long hair flying wildly around her shoulders. Lifting her hands, she pushed him in the chest. 'Get out of my house; you make me sick.'

'No.' Theo clasped both her hands in one of his and raised his other to brush his fingers through her curling black hair, tucking it behind her ear. 'Are you trying to tell me you ran out on me nine years ago because you thought I was engaged?'

'Not thought, Theo. *Knew,*' she said vehemently.

Ignoring her comment, Theo said, almost to himself, 'You lied at the airport about the pill because you assumed I was engaged, and you were jealous.'

'Jealous? Of you? Never! And I never lied,' Willow snapped, trying desperately to hang onto her anger. But the low, husky note in his voice was making it very difficult, and his strong hand keeping her wrists pressed against his hard chest wasn't helping. 'I merely said I had *heard* of the morning-after pill. How you chose to interpret it was up to you.'

She gave a short, ironic laugh. 'Dear God! I was naive. I would never have mentioned it, except I was absolutely sure I could not possibly be pregnant because you had used protection.' She lifted her eyes to his. 'A sensible precaution with your womanising lifestyle and especially as you were engaged to someone else at the time.' She tried desperately to rekindle her anger by reminding herself that Theo was a devious, cold-hearted love rat, with absolutely no morals.

For a moment Theo had almost felt sympathy for her. She had been very young, and he knew Dianne had always been fond of stretching the truth. But her sneering dig at his supposed lecherous lifestyle banished any of his finer feelings. She was still the woman who had cold-heartedly deprived him of his son. That was all he needed to know.

'Yesterday you said to me, *"I try never to dwell on the past but prefer to look to the future."* Do you remember that?' he prompted hardly, and for a long moment he studied her upturned face. Her smouldering anger mingled with a sensuality she could not disguise and was visible in the depths of her sapphire eyes.

Helpless to tear her gaze from his, Willow could feel the steady pounding of his heart through her palms. She had the wild urge to spread her fingers and trace the perfect musculature of his hard chest; to reach around his strong neck and drag his mouth back to hers again. Shocked by the intensity of her own longing, she swallowed hard. What was it about this man that he could render her speechless and a quivering mass of raw feeling without even trying?

'It is time to take your own advice, Willow, but know this...' Theo continued. 'Your future, and that of our son, is with me.' His hard, sensual mouth set in a tough line. Willow could yell at him, deny it as much as she liked, but he could feel the involuntary flexing of her fingers on his chest, could see the pulse beating in her neck, and he knew he only had to bend his head and her mouth was his for the taking.

She oozed sex appeal; she could not help herself. Theo remembered all too well that sex with her had been out of this world. He wondered, with bitter humour, how many more men had possessed her exquisite body since him. She had said only one last night. But he was no fool; in all his thirty-seven years he had rarely met a woman who admitted to having had more than one lover. Experience had taught him that one was the standard response.

But it didn't matter any more; as she was the mother of his son, her love life stopped now. He was not having his son exposed to a parade of *uncles* as some unfortunate children did in today's world. If she needed sex then he was perfectly willing to accommodate her, married or not, and he deliberately lowered his head.

She knew he was going to kiss her and to her shame her slender body tensed with anticipation. She waited, unable to take the step back her common sense was urging her to do.

CHAPTER SIX

'COOEEE, Willow,' a high-pitched voice sounded from the back garden.

'That will be Tess,' Willow murmured and Theo's dark head lifted. In a couple of strides he was leaning casually against the pine dresser at the end of the kitchen just as the back door opened.

'Hi, love, so you are up, then?' Tess put her head around the door. 'I thought I better check on you as it is almost time to collect Stephen. You looked shattered earlier.'

'Yes, thanks, Tess.' Willow smiled shakily at her friend, glad of the interruption—a momentary release of the tension that was binding her to Theo—but a second later she wasn't feeling as sure as Tess walked into the room.

'I was just in the back garden clearing out the shed, and I came across this cool-box,' she said, waving the bright red and white box in her hand. 'I thought it would come in useful for you and Stephen when you go on holiday tomorrow.'

'I'm sure it will,' Willow managed to say before another voice cut in.

'Aren't you going to introduce me to your friend, Willow, *darling?*' a deep, dark voice drawled.

Tess dropped the cool box in surprise. She hadn't noticed the man standing at the end of the kitchen until Theo strolled forward and slid a possessive arm around Willow's waist.

For a second Willow was too astonished and angry to speak. Theo's mockingly voiced 'darling' sickening her, she tried to shake off his controlling arm. But Tess appeared to notice nothing amiss as she looked up at the tall dark stranger before her, her green eyes sparkling with curiosity and pure female appreciation.

'Well, Willow has kept you quiet,' Tess exclaimed as Theo gave her a brilliant smile. 'I'm Tess, her neighbour.' She held out her hand and Theo took it. But instead of shaking it, he raised it elegantly to his lips before gently releasing it.

'It is a real pleasure to meet you, Tess. I am Theo Kadros, a very old friend of Willow's.' He cast a glittering sidelong glance at Willow's flushed and furious face. 'Isn't that right, *darling?*' His fingers digging into her waist dictated her reply.

'Yes,' Willow grated between clenched teeth, knowing that if he said 'darling' once more she would thump him. She didn't know what Theo was up to, but he was up to something and she knew she would not like it. He was quite deliberately giving Tess the impression that they were already intimate friends.

As for Tess. Willow wondered what on earth was the matter with her? As a happily married woman she should have more sense than to be taken in by Theo's brand of sophisticated charm. Instead she was flirting with him, quite outrageously.

'Now I know why she wanted to get back to bed so eagerly this morning,' Tess said. 'You were waiting for her.' She laughed up into his smiling eyes, and, finally looking at Willow, adding, 'You dark horse. I asked you about Mr Carlavitch but you never mentioned you already had a man in tow who was even more handsome, or that you had brought him home with you,' she teased.

'I did—' was as far as she got in denying Tess's assumption, before Theo cut in.

'I am the man she and Stephen are going on holiday with. Hopefully that will be tonight rather than tomorrow. That is if we can impose on you again, Tess, to look after the cottage while we are away?'

'Oh, I will be delighted.' Tess's attention immediately diverted from Willow back to Theo. 'I am always telling Willow that she doesn't get out enough or go anywhere, like other girls of her age. Stephen is a lovely boy, and she is a great mum, but she tries to be a dad to him as well. What Willow is badly in need of is a few more adult pursuits.'

Willow's mouth fell open in shock at her friend's treachery. Her lips moved but no words came out.

'I agree and fully intend to change all that,' Theo said smoothly. 'For a highly intelligent and successful woman, I am always saying that Willow spends far too much time locked away with her books.'

'Exactly what I have told her.' Tess beamed, and Willow exploded.

'Now just a minute.' They were talking about her as if she didn't exist. She expected this kind of behaviour from Theo, but not from Tess. 'I am not going anywhere with Theo, and, Tess, you have got it all wrong.'

'As wrong as the buttons on your dress, I suppose.' Tess grinned. 'I don't think so.' And she burst out laughing.

Willow glanced down at herself, and her face turned a fiery red with embarrassment. 'Oh, my God!' she exclaimed. The top two buttonholes of her dress were empty, and the first button was slipped into the third hole, revealing much more of one breast than was ever intended. 'You could have told me,' she yelled at a grinning Theo, and she wanted to reach out and slap the smile off his face. Instead she began hastily refastening the front of her dress correctly. 'I made lunch and everything,' she groaned with embarrassment.

'Oh, will you just look at the time? It's twenty past three already,' Tess cried. 'Got to go, love, and you will have to go and collect Stephen soon. Drop the cottage keys in later when you leave and have a great holiday.' She shot out of the back door before Willow could stop her. It was the last straw for Willow.

Elbowing Theo hard in the ribs, she spun out of his hold. 'What the hell do you think you are playing at?' she demanded, glaring up at his strong, autocratic face. 'How dare you come into my house and lie and embarrass me in front of my friend? Who the hell do you think you are?' She screamed at him, her eyes flashing fire. 'I am going absolutely nowhere with you.'

'There isn't time for a temper tantrum,' Theo said, coolly glancing down at the slim platinum watch on his wrist, and then back to her flushed, furious face. 'Unless you intend to leave our son standing alone at the school gates,' he drawled sardonically. 'But then again that would give my lawyers more ammunition if it came to a custody case.'

'You, you…' she spluttered. She realised that he might be right, damn him. She stared back at him, her brilliant blue eyes glittering with fury and frustration. Her fingers curled into fists at her sides to prevent them developing a will of their own and slugging the damn man. That would go down well in a court of law—a mother given to fits of violence. Unable to hold Theo's steel-hard gaze, Willow looked down at the floor, teeth catching at her lower lip. She could not afford to give this man any more ammunition to beat her with.

'I'll go and collect Stephen, and you can wait here,' she said with what composure she could muster, and, turning, walked out of the kitchen and headed down the hall.

A large hand closed around her elbow. 'No. I will come with you, and you can fill me in on what exactly you have told Stephen about me before I meet him.'

With a defeated shrug of her slender shoulders, Willow sighed, and, pushing open the front door, walked outside. She glanced up the road past the ominous black car parked outside her house. Stephen would be out of school in minutes and she had run out of time.

Theo stopped and turned her towards him, his night-black eyes zeroing in on her. 'I'm waiting, Willow, and I want the truth.'

'I told Stephen the truth,' she said bluntly. 'I met his father when I was very young, and we became close. I left to go and stay with my mother in India, and when I discovered I was pregnant and returned to London the man had vanished.' She shot him a vitriolic look. 'I went to your house but something called British Land Ltd was converting it. As for the rest of the story, I told Stephen you had married someone else before he was born. Again the truth because I saw the pictures of your wedding in a flashy magazine. End of story.' Her own expression steely, she looked straight into his black eyes, daring him to deny it.

Theo felt as if he had been hit by a ten-ton truck. 'You came looking for me?'

'Only because my mum said it was the right thing to do. I already knew I was wasting my time,' she drawled derisively, and set off once more along the lane to the school.

His strong face grim with the gravity of thoughts that he could no longer deny, Theo followed along behind her. Willow was telling the truth, she had looked for him, or how else could she have known the name 'British Land Ltd', which was a subsidiary of one of his own companies. And he remembered all too well his wedding to Dianne in

New York six months later, and the extravagant magazine spread of the event that Dianne had insisted on.

He looked at Willow marching along in front of him now, and he was reminded of the very first time he'd seen her. Her marvellous black hair falling in silken waves down her back. She had been quite scantily clad then, and he had been recklessly determined to have her. No thought had been in his head other than a casual affair. He had only just escaped the tightening clutches of a very determined Dianne. So he had taken Willow to his bed, and then been furiously angry when he'd discovered the following morning that she had left him. He had been almost apoplectic when he had caught her later at the airport.

He squared his broad shoulders. Maybe some of the fault was his, he recognised, and he meant to tell her so. He increased his stride to move alongside her, and then he saw his son.

'Hey, Mum,' a boyish voice cried and Theo was struck dumb as Willow dashed forward.

'Stephen, you know you are not supposed to leave the school yard alone,' she remonstrated, a smile twitching the corners of her lush lips as she looked down at him.

'Ah, Mum, I could see you coming so Miss Lamb said it was okay.'

'Okay then this time. But just remember next term, when you go to the middle school in town, you must wait for me.'

'Yes, I know.' His young face creased in a frown. 'But why is that man following you, Mum?' he demanded, scowling warily up at Theo, who had stopped at her side.

Having completely forgotten Theo for the moment, Willow was suddenly brought back to reality with a vengeance. She glanced fearfully up at him, terrified at what he might say. But his entire concentration was focussed on the small boy staring warily up at him. She could see that his shock over the discovery that he was a father had been replaced by a burning desire to know his child, the emotion in his dark, intense eyes unmistakable.

She saw his hands clench at his sides, as if it would stop him reaching out for the boy, and she sensed his bitter frustration. It was there in the taut lines of his powerful body, the proud tilt of his dark head. For the first time since meeting Theo again, her heart went out to him, and she actually felt compassion for him. She had always had Stephen, and his unconditional love in her life. But Theo...

'Who are you?' Stephen demanded bravely, and his hand reached out to seek hers. Looking back down at her son, Willow felt her heart flood with pride and love. At only eight he was already her protector.

'Why are you following my mum?'

'It's all right, Stephen.' Willow looked from one to the other, and Theo caught her upward gaze, his eyes blazing for a second with killing enmity into hers. He was never going to forgive her for denying him the boy, and any compassion she had for him quickly vanished.

'What your mother is trying to say,' Theo stated dropping to his haunches so his face was near Stephen's level, 'is that I am Theo Kadros, a very old friend of hers. I met your mother yesterday in London, and we had a drink together. Then I saw a photograph of you and your mother in the newspaper this morning and I thought it would be nice to visit you both. Your name is Stephen, isn't it? I may call you Stephen?' he queried with a tentative smile. 'And you can call me Theo.' Extending a strong hand, he added, 'Shake on it.'

With all the fickleness of youth, Stephen smiled back, his eyes, so like his father's, dancing with excitement as he took the hand offered. 'Sure, Theo, but did you really see my photo in the newspaper?'

'Yes, of course, and it was excellent.'

'Great.' Stephen spun back towards Willow. 'See, Mum, I told you the reporter said I would be in the paper.' Smiling back at Theo, he asked, 'Have you still got the paper? Can I see it?'

'Please,' Willow prompted, falling back on her good manners, when all else failed, as usual. She supposed she should be relieved that at least Theo had not said you could call me Dad. But her relief was short-lived...

'Of course you can, it is in my car.' Theo smiled and rose to his feet. 'It is parked just outside your door. I will show you it if you like.'

'Yes, please.' Stephen swung around. 'Come on, Mum, let's go.'

Willow had no choice but to walk back home with Stephen skipping along between her and Theo. She glanced at Theo over the top of the boy's head and she went white at the outraged fury in the dark, expressive eyes that clashed for a moment with her own. He might be charming to Stephen but his charm certainly did not extend to her. The black cloud that had hung over her since meeting him yesterday suddenly seemed to envelop her in an all-encompassing dread for the future.

When Willow was faced with a problem she did what she always did: resorted to cool politeness and mundane chores. Procrastination could have been her middle name, as Tess was often fond of telling her, and she was right. So she left Stephen and Theo eulogising over the massive Mercedes and went into the house to make the tea.

Safe in the kitchen, she put the kettle on to boil. Staring at the table, she wondered how long their cosy routine would continue, and she knew she had to do something.

And this time she knew procrastination was not an option. She squeezed her eyes shut in an attempt to stop the tears falling and cursed all over again for stupidly exposing her little family to the press. She must have been mad…

Theo Kadros was not the type of man to be content with an occasional visit to his son. She had caught the longing, the possessive gleam in his eyes when he had first seen Stephen. He had hid his anger well from the boy, but she was under no illusion. He wanted him, and, as he had said earlier, he did not have to take her. But a court case, a battle for custody over Stephen…could she face it?

Yes, damn it! She could, and she brushed the moisture from her eyes. Whatever else she was, she was not a coward, and she was not going to let a man whom she had only met once turn her into one.

For her writing she did a lot of research; it was essential to have one's facts straight. It was way past time she got back into professional mode, instead of being led around by her emotions. And with that in mind she went straight to the telephone on the kitchen wall. She quickly dialled the number of her lawyer, Mr Swinburn.

Five minutes later she put the phone down feeling much more confident. She had explained her problem, and been reassured.

A man she had only met once; a man she had gone looking for to tell him he was to be a father, only to discover the man in question had married someone else. A man who had never met the boy until he was eight and had never paid a penny to support the boy. He didn't really have a leg to stand on in Mr Swinburn's view. As for the expense, he assured Willow with the money coming in from her writing she could afford it, and he foresaw no problem at all.

Then it hit her. What on earth was she thinking of leaving Stephen alone with Theo? He could whisk him away in an instant, and with a gasp of panic Willow shot back out of the house. Just in time, as she saw Stephen about to step into Theo's car.

'Stephen, come here this minute, your tea is ready,' she shouted.

'Oh, Mum. Theo was just going to take me for a drive. Can't it wait?'

'No,' she declared and, trying not to look as panicked as she felt, she walked down the path and grabbed Stephen's hand. 'Later, maybe.'

'Your mother is right, Stephen.' Much to her amazement Theo backed her up with a grin for Stephen. But he flicked her a cold glance of cutting perception, before turning his attention back to Stephen. 'First tea, and then how about we all go for a drive to Exeter, where my aircraft is waiting?'

'Wow, you have an aeroplane,' Stephen exclaimed, his eyes wide like saucers. 'How cool! Can I see it?'

'Yes, of course, in fact you can fly in it. I know you and your mum had planned to go on holiday tomorrow. But how about if we all go tonight instead? You can stay with me at my villa in Greece.' Lifting his dark head, his black eyes gleaming with triumph and something else Willow could not name, he went on. 'Instead of—where was it you were going again, Willow?'

She had never mentioned going on holidays to Theo, and then she remembered Tess and her big mouth, and groaned inwardly. He hadn't been joking when he'd asked Tess to look after the house. Things could not get much worse. But they did...

'We usually go to Falmouth. And then to France,' Stephen answered for her. 'Mum was going to look for my dad. But that can wait a bit longer, I'd much rather fly to Greece.'

'Come in for your tea,' Willow snapped, suddenly terrified what Theo would say next. But her worst fear was realised.

'This is your lucky day, Stephen.' Theo placed a hand on his small shoulder and looked straight into his excited eyes. 'Because your mother has already found your father. I am your dad, and we are all going to Greece to meet your grandmother and aunty and cousins.'

Willow wanted the ground to open and swallow her up. She went as white as a sheet, and her legs turned to jelly. She looked at Theo with wide, wounded blue eyes, incapable of saying a word. How could he blurt the information out so brutally? A strong arm curved around her waist, and he smiled down into her eyes.

'Isn't that right, Willow?'

'Yes,' she whispered. Stephen flung his arms around her thighs, and looked up at her with such adoration, she had to blink.

'Thanks, Mum, I always knew you would find him one day. I just knew it,' he declared in delight. His absolute faith in her made Willow feel about two inches tall, and Theo's sardonic smile simply compounded her guilt.

CHAPTER SEVEN

CURSING silently beneath her breath, Willow paced up and down the huge bedroom illuminated by a single bedside lamp. She was seething with resentment and much too furious to sleep, the rumpled bed testament to the fact. It was all the fault of one man: Theo *mighty* Kadros.

He had swept back into her life like a cyclone. Stephen was sleeping in the next room along the hall, and she still could not get her head around the fact that her son had taken one look at Theo and had accepted him. No, not just accepted him, he actually hero-worshipped his father within hours of meeting him.

She was hurt and, yes, jealous, she freely admitted, and absolutely flaming mad. None of these emotions conducive to sleep. Willow slumped down on the edge of the huge bed, and wanted to cry her eyes out.

After Theo's declaration this afternoon that he was Stephen's father, and her son's unbridled joy at the news, events had overtaken her completely. Knowing only too well she was unwilling to upset her son, Theo had used emotional blackmail of the worst kind to get his own way. He had given her no chance to refuse and before she'd known it they had been in a car heading towards Exeter airport, and later boarding Theo's luxurious jet.

Unable to relax on the flight to Greece, she had struggled to make sense of the emotional roller-coaster ride of the past thirty-six hours. From the elation she had felt at winning the award and securing the film contract, to her shock at seeing Theo again, to another kind of elation—the way

she had felt in Theo's arms. But then there had been the
utter horror of a dangerously angry Theo turning up on her
doorstep and demanding to see her son.

Finally watching Theo patiently explaining every intri-
cate bit of the aircraft to Stephen, noting the easy interac-
tion between father and son, she had been forced to accept
that Theo Kadros was now a permanent part of their life.

The arrival at the villa, set high up in the hills outside
Athens, two hours earlier had been fraught with tension. A
butler by the name of Takis had welcomed them and shown
them into a very elegant lounge. But Willow's most vivid
image had been of Theo's mother, small and dark and very
elegant, introducing herself and showering lots of hugs and
kisses on Stephen. She had politely asked Willow if she
would like a drink, and something to eat, but Willow had
given a rather stilted refusal using the excuse that it was
very late, and all the while Theo had stood by saying nothing.

But then he hadn't needed to say anything, she thought
on another sizzling burst of rage. He had her and Stephen
right where he wanted them.

Finally Mrs Kadros had swept a sleepy Stephen into her
arms and insisted on carrying him up to his room. After
watching Willow put Stephen to bed, she had shown
Willow to her room next door, and wished her goodnight,
saying they could all talk in the morning.

Talk… That was a laugh, she thought bitterly, rising to
her feet, too restless to sit still. Who was going to listen to
what she wanted for Stephen? Certainly not Theo, and like
any mother Mrs Kadros was bound to support her own son.

Walking to the huge windows that opened onto a balcony, Willow stared out at the night sky and wondered
fearfully what the future had in store. She was in a house

full of people but had never felt so totally alone in her whole life.

'I thought you might still be awake.'

She had not heard the door open but she heard the husky-voiced drawl and spun around to stare in disbelief. 'Get out of my room,' she snapped as she watched Theo close the door softly behind him and turn the key. Something she should have done herself, she realised only too late. 'Haven't you done enough damage for one day, Theo?' she said bitterly.

'Be quiet.' He moved towards her, and it was then that it dawned on her that he was wearing only a short towelling robe that exposed his broad chest and long legs. She was pretty sure that he was naked beneath it, as was she in her skimpy cotton nightshirt…

Her heart lurched and she was furious at herself, at him and at the whole damn world. She saw the lazy sensuality in his dark eyes as he stopped an arm's reach away, and the sheer gall of the man staggered her. He had already charmed her son, and she was obviously next on his agenda.

She sucked in a furious breath. 'Don't you dare tell me to be quiet, you no-good, manipulative swine,' she threw at him, her eyes flashing blue fire. 'What kind of lowlife are you that you would use a small boy to blackmail me into coming here? What kind of so-called father would do a thing like that?' she challenged him, her anger laced with scorn.

Theo had kept an iron control on his emotions for the last twenty-four hours. He had told his mother an abridged version of what had happened and then spent the last hour simply watching his son sleep. Filled with an overwhelming love for the boy, he had realised he would give his life to protect him. On that thought it had struck him that Willow must also feel the same, and how afraid she must be feeling with his threat of court action hanging over her head.

Leaving his son's room, he had walked past Willow's and seen the glimmer of light under the door. It had occurred to him to reassure her that he had no intention of taking her to court over the boy and he was sure that they could come to a suitable arrangement that would be beneficial to all three of them.

But looking at her now standing with her back to the window, the slip of cotton she was wearing barely reaching her thighs, her glorious hair tumbling around her shoulders in wanton disarray, the expression on her beautiful face one of angry contempt—he changed his mind. She was looking at him as if he were something she needed to scrape off her shoe. Any finer feelings that had been induced by visiting his son's bedside were quickly forgotten.

Cold fury glittered in his dark eyes. All arrogant Greek male, he allowed no one to disrespect him, man or woman, and certainly not this woman. She had so cruelly deprived him of his child, and yet she dared to question his ability as a father. What chance had she given him? None.

He wanted to tear her limb from limb. Her full lips that he had tasted not nearly enough were twisted in a contemptuous smile. Angrily he studied her, his eyes raking over her body. The thin white slip she was wearing was almost transparent, moulding her firm high breasts and narrow waist. The fine rounded curves of her hips and the dark shadow of feminine body hair almost visible through the flimsy fabric. Damn it! She was enough to tempt a saint, and he was no saint, as an instant stirring in his groin forcibly reminded him.

It was then that a scenario worthy of his Greek heritage crossed his mind. His dark eyes narrowed with implacable resolve. In that moment he made his decision for the future of his son and this beautiful scornful creature standing before him.

'What, no response?' Willow jeered into the lengthening silence. The air between them sizzled with tension and she dragged an angry, if slightly unsteady, breath into her suddenly oxygen-starved lungs. Theo stepped closer, his dark features rigid as he gave her a look of such cynical sexual appraisal she reeled in shock for a breathless, heart-stopping moment. Every self-protective instinct she possessed was urging her to step back, but she refused to be cowed by his intimidating presence.

'You ask what kind of father?' he prompted scathingly, his eyes like black ice biting accusingly into hers. 'The kind that has been deprived of his son for years,' he hissed with sibilant softness, his hand snaking around her, trapping one arm against him and drawing her closer. 'The kind whose child is eight years old and does not speak one word of his father's language.'

She could not deny his words, and the sudden contact with his hard, muscular body sent the blood pounding through her veins and she panicked. She tried to twist from his hold. 'No,' she cried but she was too late. His hand slipped right around her waist, and caught her other wrist in his long fingers, melding her to him from chest to thigh. Ignoring her muttered negative, he continued with raw venom.

'The kind who has had to watch his mother cry tears of joy and regret that her husband never lived to see the boy.' His free hand came up to burrow under the heavy fall of her hair and twist it around his wrist. He pulled back her head, and she knew she was in deep, deep trouble.

'You owe me, Willow, eight long years, and now is my time to collect.'

She stared up into his eyes and trembled at the fury that

glittered in the inky depths. Willow was also aware of a much more basic emotion that she could not fail to recognise. 'No, Theo. Let go of me, or I will scream the place down.' Her voice shook with fear as she said it, and her body responded similarly as the heat of him enveloped her. The familiar scent of him tantalised her nostrils, and the imprint of his warm, hard body against her own sent her pulse rate into overdrive.

'Scream all you like, the walls are a foot thick,' he mocked. His face was a taut mask of rigidly controlled anger. 'You had the first eight years of Stephen's life, and I am having the next eight—legally.' He tilted her head further back, his glittering eyes boring down into hers with implacable determination. 'We will marry, and at sixteen Stephen will be of an age to choose between us. Then we can divorce.' His dark head bent, and the air caught in her throat as his warm breath brushed her ear. 'But first, Willow, I am going to make you burn for denying me,' he threatened in a deep, sexually explicit drawl.

She almost admitted that she already was, so overwhelming were the sensations shooting through her, imprisoned in his powerful hold. But she choked back the words; he was the enemy and she hated him. What sort of man discussed a divorce virtually in the same sentence as mentioning marriage? She wriggled against him and tried to lift her hands to push him away, but to no avail.

'Don't bother trying to escape.' He gave a husky laugh holding her with ease. 'You want this as much as me, and you can deny it as much as you like but you will never convince me otherwise. I was the man you chose as a teenager to initiate you in the pleasures of sex, and your lovely body remembers me however much you try to forget. And my body remembers you, Willow,' he confessed softly. 'Has painfully done so for years.'

Stunned, Willow stared at him and saw the faint flush developing across his high cheekbones. What was he saying? That he remembered her, even missed her? No. That couldn't be true. She might have had a chance of resisting him if she had not been so confused.

But instead she felt the moist warmth of his tongue trace the delicate whorls of her ear and trail down her throat, where his mouth closed over the madly beating pulse in her neck. 'No, Theo,' she choked, and she was stunned again by the incredible hunger that shook her to the depths of her being. Her neck arched helplessly in sensual response to his touch.

'Yes, say my name.' His hand at her waist diverted to slip beneath the hem of her slip and glide up over her naked thigh, and she gasped in shock at the intimacy. Then he claimed her mouth with a devastating expertise.

Pressed against the impressive length of him, his tongue delving between her parted lips, she made a weak attempt to struggle free. But his hand splayed intimately across the swell of her hips, urging her into the hard, grinding power of his thighs while his mouth, hard and hungry, impelled her into a more fervent response.

Willow collapsed like a pack of cards, the white-hot flames of desire consuming her and obliterating any thought of resistance from her mind. Her hands of their own volition stroked up under the lapels of his robe and curved around his broad shoulders. Her intimate action caused his robe to fall open and she felt the rock-hard power of his arousal against her stomach. Her whole body shook with excitement and instinctively she squirmed against him.

His tongue explored the moist heat of her mouth and stroked across the sensitive roof, creating a thousand tiny electric shocks through every nerve in her body. Willow moaned, her fingers sliding up into his sleek black hair.

Greedy for him, she bit down on his bottom lip and he responded in kind. He unfurled her hair from his wrist and raked his long fingers through it, smoothing the silken waves down the length of her back. He lifted his head and she saw the barely controlled passion in the smouldering depths of his eyes; she let her hands stroke down his magnificent chest with tactile delight, her fingers lingering in his soft, curling body hair.

He said something guttural in Greek, and, suddenly stepping back, he freed her.

'No,' Willow groaned, not to stop him this time, but quite the reverse. Then in one deft move he wrenched her shirt over her head. Her eyes flew wide open, and clashed with his smouldering black. For a second she questioned what she was doing, standing naked before him, but with a shrug his robe fell from his broad shoulders, and she was spellbound. The sight of his incredible bronzed body caused her to feel an intense awe and a burning desire to touch him. She reached out, but Theo caught her hand, and spun her up into his arms.

'Not yet, my beauty,' he said and moved to swiftly put her down on the bed. 'Later you can touch, but first I am going to make you burn.'

She should have felt afraid, but it had been exactly like this the first time they had made love. He'd only had to kiss her and she had lost all her inhibitions and gone wild in his arms. Looking up at him now, she knew why nothing had changed. He had been her first and only lover, and the same fascination she had felt as a teenager kept her still now. Her glittering blue eyes roamed over his magnificent body with pure female appreciation for what he was—a perfect male. Tall and sleek, muscled with not an ounce of fat, his skin gleamed like oiled teak. He was wide of shoulder, broad of chest, with a washboard stomach. An intriguing pattern of body hair, curling across his chest, guided the eye down his long body like an arrow to frame his now fiercely aroused sex. She had never really had the chance to study his masculine form quite so intently before, youthful embarrassment had played a part, but now she had no such qualms and—quite simply—he took her breath away.

'Seen enough?' Theo drawled, and, slightly red-faced, she lifted her eyes to his and she caught the gleam of masculine satisfaction. In one swift movement he was beside her on the bed.

Willow trembled at the brush of his long naked body against her own. His strong hands clasped hers and, raising them to his mouth, he kissed and licked each palm, sending pulsating waves of pleasure through her tender flesh. He laced his long fingers through hers and, leaning over her, pinned her hands above her head.

Theo stared down at her, fiercely battling against the intense urge to take her hard, hot and instantly. At last he had Willow where and how he wanted her, and he was determined to savour every single inch of her; to prolong the pleasure to the very last second of sense. Her brilliant blue eyes were smoky with desire, her incredibly sexy mouth slightly swollen and pouting, her firm white breasts...too tempting to ignore any longer... He bent his head and licked each rigid nipple, before returning to capture her mouth with his own.

For Willow it was like being struck by lightning. A fierce wave of heat flared from her breasts to her thighs, and she quaked with need. Her tongue duelled with his in a greedy passion she could not control. Did not want to.

She felt his hands running up and down the soft underside of her arms, his great body pressing into her. She was amazed that she had never known an arm could be an erotic zone, but she did now. Every inch of her body became an erotic zone where this man was concerned, she thought wonderingly as his tongue plunged inside her mouth again in intimation of the sexual act.

This was what her body had been craving for years, and all her doubts and guilty feelings were swept aside. She was lost in her own feverish response to the awesome sensations he evoked in her body, which had been for far too long sexually deprived. She strained up against him, and tried to pull her hands free; she desperately wanted to touch him, to explore him.

Theo reared up and looked down at her with hot, dark eyes. 'Now it is my turn to look at you.' He freed her hand, but only for an instant as he again enclosed both of hers in one of his. 'I have dreamt of doing this for years,' he grated and his hand slid around her throat. 'Having you naked and hot beneath me, your glorious hair spread over the pillow.' And slowly his hand traced down over her breast, rolling the rigid tip between his finger and thumb.

Arrows of delight shot through her, every cell in her body attuned to his touch. When his mouth replaced his fingers by suckling on each rigid nipple in turn she gasped in delirious pleasure.

'You like that,' he husked, his dark eyes molten pools of desire capturing hers.

'Yes, oh, yes,' she said on a moaning sigh of pure delight. 'But, please…' she tried to pull her hands free '…I want to touch you.'

He shook his dark head. 'No, Willow. If you touch me it will be over in a flash,' he declared throatily. He carefully inserted one long leg between her thighs and, leaning over her, he stroked slowly over the aching mound of one breast. Then slowly his hand moved down to the indentation of her waist and across her flat stomach, and inched lower to cup her sex and he stopped. His head lowered to once more claim her mouth, his tongue invading the moist interior with a passionate, possessive intensity that had her writhing hotly beneath him and instinctively parting her legs wider, burning for his intimate touch.

'I want to watch you,' Theo rasped. His lips trailed down her throat to her achingly aroused nipples, and he teased them with his teeth and tongue. He lifted his head. 'I want to see the passion in your incredible eyes.' His black glance seared into hers as he slipped a long finger between her trembling thighs and found the velvet fold of flesh and the centre of her pleasure, hot and wet and waiting for him.

Willow closed her eyes, a low moan escaping her as he caressed her with delicate strokes, slowly driving her wild. She shuddered with the force of her need, a want so achingly exquisite it was almost pain, and she cried out his name.

'Yes,' Theo grated. 'Say my name, Willow,' and he touched the tip of his tongue to each pert breast. 'I'm going to give you more pleasure than your wildest fantasies, until you can think of no other man but me, and I am going to enjoy every second.'

Willow might have been threatened by his words but she had given her body over to this powerful man. Her back arched off the bed. 'Please, Theo.' She pressed up into his hand, and felt his great body shake. He was as aroused as she was, his bronzed skin damp with sweat and his breathing ragged. Suddenly her hands were free, and wildly she reached for him, her fingers raking down his broad back as he moved between her thighs. Her head fell back and she stared up into his hard face with dazzling, hungry eyes.

A spasm of raw emotion flashed across his taut, dark features. 'God...I have to have you,' he growled. 'I can't wait.'

Willow didn't want him to, and with a wantonness she

had never known she bit down on his chest, her teeth grazing a hard, masculine nipple, her tongue licking the salt from his skin, and her hand reaching down to touch him— take him. She was oblivious to everything but the scent, the taste and the tremendous burning, quivering hunger she felt for him. Theo knocked her hand away and, gripping her hips, he lifted her, and with the first fierce thrust of his manhood deep into her hot, tight body Willow cried out, her long legs wrapping around his waist.

He stilled for a moment and she looked at him with fevered pleading blue eyes, her inner muscles clenching around him poised on the agonising brink of orgasm. His face was a rigid mask of pure tension.

'Are you burning now, Willow?'

She didn't answer him, didn't need to as, with a primitive instinct as old as time, she dug her nails into his satin-smooth skin and gave a wickedly wanton upward thrust of her hips. His control snapped, and he plunged hard and deep with a driving intensity that tipped Willow over the edge in a tumultuous release. She clung to him as wave after wave of incredible sensations hit her and she cried out his name. Then the world fell away as his great body also shuddered violently in the awesome pleasure of his own climax.

For a long moment they lay joined together, Theo with his face buried in the curve of her throat and shoulder, and the only sound in the room their ragged breathing. Willow, still trembling in the aftermath, realised she was clinging to him. What had she done? a tiny voice of conscience queried in her bemused brain. But she had no time to ponder this question as incredibly she felt Theo growing again inside her and they did it all over again...

This time more slowly, silently. A mutual exploration of the senses, where time had no meaning. All that mattered was the two sweat-slicked bodies gliding together, moving over and under with exploring hands and mouths, and ever-increasing passion until they blended again into one mutual, heart-stopping climax.

A long time later Theo lifted up on his elbow, and stared down at her. Damn it! How did this dark-haired witch do it to him? She infuriated and inflamed him into the rashest of actions. He had not meant to lose control, but he had…so much so that no thought of protection had entered his head.

His jet-black eyes roamed over her flushed face, and he reached out a hand and brushed some stray tendrils of her raven hair back from her cheek. Her love-swollen lips parted in a beautiful smile and she looked almost innocent as his gaze moved down the long, slender length of her body.

He must be going weak in the head… There was nothing innocent about her. He could still feel the effect of her incredible long legs wrapped around him. He had thought she was sex on legs the very first time he had seen her, and she had been everything he remembered and much more. She was a perfect fit for him, she was fire and light in his arms, and he grimaced. Willow was an incredibly sensuous woman, she couldn't help herself, and he suddenly wondered how many other men there had been in the past nine years.

He jerked up into a sitting position, not liking where his thoughts were taking him. It was enough for him that he had her now. 'We will marry before the end of the week,' he grated, and leapt off the bed to stand frowning down at her. 'We will tell everyone in the morning, a small civil ceremony—'

'Wait a minute,' Willow cut in, shock cutting through the euphoria of the past hour. She sat up and hastily pulled the cotton sheet over her breasts, suddenly embarrassingly

aware of her nakedness. Not that Theo seemed to be bothered, she thought as he stood towering over her apparently
totally at ease with his nudity. 'I never agreed to marry
you, Theo.'

Theo did not even attempt to argue the point. He did not
need to. He never missed a chance to turn a mistake into
a success in the business world, and he instantly grasped
the opportunity to do the same now in his private life.

'You don't have a choice any more, Willow.' His black
eyes, a gleam of mocking triumph visible in their inky
depths, clashed with her stunned blue. 'One illegitimate
child is enough for any family, and as you may have been
aware we did not use any protection,' he emphasised in a
deep cynical drawl. 'You have no chance of getting the
morning-after pill here so, unless you are already on the
pill…?' He let the words hang in the air, not needing to
say any more; the shocked expression on her lovely face
said it all.

Ashen-faced, Willow stared up at him. 'You bastard,' she
swore. 'You did it deliberately. But it makes no difference.'
She had managed to raise Stephen on her own and she
could, if she had to, do it again. 'I am not going to marry
you.'

One dark brow arched sardonically before he turned to
pick up his robe from the edge of the bed. He slipped it on
and tied the belt firmly around his waist.

He had just dropped a bombshell and then simply turned
his back on her. Frightened and furious, Willow yelled,
'Answer me, damn you.'

Slowly he turned back to face her, his handsome face
devoid of all expression. 'You never asked a question,' he
said with a dismissive shrug of his shoulders. 'Feel free to
believe what you like, Willow, but know this—' the eyes
that met hers were cold and as hard as jet '—we will marry

next week. I told you before you owe me eight years, and I meant it.' Her blood chilled at the icy determination in his tone. 'You and Stephen will be staying here in Greece after the wedding so the boy has a chance to learn his own language and something of his heritage. We can discuss the minor details in the morning.'

The full enormity of what he had just said hit her like a punch in the stomach. The eager attentive lover of moments ago had changed into an autocratic tyrant laying down the law as if he were King. But what really frightened Willow was the knowledge that Theo might very well be right. She could be pregnant again with his child. Dear heaven, the only other time Theo had touched her Stephen had been the result, even with protection! But then common sense and maturity prevailed. She had finished her period only three days ago, so unless she was the unluckiest woman on the planet she should be safe. She was determined that she was not going to be forced into marriage by any man.

'Get some sleep—you look worn out.'

'And whose fault is that?' she slashed back.

'Mine, of course,' he drawled with a sardonic lift of an ebony eyebrow. 'But don't pretend you didn't enjoy it, you were with me every step of the way, and unless you want to continue where we left off I suggest you rest. We will talk in the morning.'

'There is nothing to talk about,' she shot back furiously. 'You can't make me marry you and I won't,' and she picked up the pillow and threw it at him.

He fielded it with one hand and gave a short derisive laugh, totally ignoring her vehement refusal. 'Keep your passion for the marriage bed, Willow,' and, spinning on his heel, he left.

CHAPTER EIGHT

A CHEERFUL sound of raised voices and laughter broke through Willow's deep sleep. Yawning, she opened her eyes, and just as quickly closed them, dazzled by the light streaming into the room. Slowly she opened them again and looked around the sunlit room, and groaned as she remembered where she was, and why.

The sound of splashing water followed by Stephen's voice screaming with delight simply made her feel worse. She suddenly remembered in all too vivid detail what she had done in this bed last night with Theo.

Oh, my God! She groaned, and rolled over and buried her face in the pillows. How could she have been so weak as to fall into his arms again like a sex-starved fool? She could never face Theo again, but she was going to have to, for Stephen's sake if nothing else.

She must have overslept, not so surprising as she had barely slept for the past two days. With a heavy sigh Willow rolled over and swung her legs over the side of the bed and realised she was naked. Her first thought was to dive back under the cover, but much as she would like to hide away in her room all day it wasn't an option. She was going to have to face Theo and his family, and she had a horrible feeling it was going to be a long, traumatic day.

Picking her nightshirt off the floor, she slipped it back on and crossed to the window. Pushing open the glass doors, she stepped out onto the balcony and gasped in pleasure at the beautiful view. Pine-clad hills undulated like green waves down to a sparkling blue sea in the distance.

'Hey, Mum, you're up. Do you want to watch me dive?'

She glanced down over the balcony and gasped again as she saw her son, clad in his swimming trunks, fling himself headlong into the deep blue waters of an Olympic-length swimming pool. She waited with bated breath for him to surface and breathed a sigh of relief when the sun gleamed off his sleek black hair. 'Well done,' she cried. 'But you should not be in the water...' Alone, she meant to say, but then she saw Theo appear at the side of the pool and extend a long arm to haul Stephen out and onto his feet beside him, and she lost her breath again.

Theo tilted his dark head back and looked up at her. 'Sorry if we woke you. But it is after nine. Breakfast is being served on the terrace, come and join us.'

'Yes...' she murmured, unable to tear her eyes away from his tall, lithe body. He was almost naked except for a pair of black bathing trunks that did little more than cup his sex. Her cheeks flaming with embarrassment, she hastily lifted her eyes to his and swallowed hard.

The dark eyes that met hers were gleaming with an unconcealed mockery; he knew exactly how she was feeling. 'Was that a yes, Willow? We didn't hear you.'

'Yes, okay,' she cried and shot back into the bedroom, her heart pounding like a sledgehammer in her chest. Seeing him standing there in the bright sunshine, every bronzed muscle and sinew clearly on display, she was vividly reminded of last night. She tried to blame the sudden rush of heat in her body on the hot sun, and headed for the *ensuite* bathroom to cool down.

A quick cold shower, and she would feel much better. Ten minutes later, stepping out of the shower, she caught a glimpse of her naked body in the long wall mirror. She stopped and straightened up. She could fool herself no longer. She doubted if even the icy water of the Arctic Ocean could freeze out the way Theo made her feel.

She studied her own reflection; her lips were still slightly swollen from his kisses, and the small bruises on the pale skin of her breasts and other parts of her body a physical reminder of his passion.

Just thinking about it now made her stomach curl and colour flood her face. Grabbing a towel, she wrapped it tightly around her body. Her own innate honesty forced her to acknowledge it was not solely Theo's passion to blame. Despising her own weakness at reacting so instantly to his touch did not alter the fact she had played a very active part in the proceedings, and had enjoyed every second of their lovemaking.

No... Love didn't come into the equation, she amended, and walked back into the bedroom. It was sex, nothing more, and she would do well to remember that. Whatever the future had in store, and at the moment it looked pretty grim, Theo Kadros was not the sort of man to fall in love with. He had women by the score and already had one divorce behind him. The only reason he wanted Willow was for Stephen and it made her more determined than ever not to marry him.

She glanced around the elegant bedroom, and noticed that a tray with coffee had appeared, and her suitcase seemed to have vanished. She drank a cup of coffee and felt marginally better; finding a bra and briefs in the top drawer of a tallboy, she slipped them on. Then she opened the first of two huge antique wardrobes standing against the far wall. She grimaced at the sight of the few clothes hanging there. She had packed for a fun week in Cornwall, a couple of pairs of shorts and two bikinis. These clothes would be a waste of time here, because as much as she would love to have a swim she did not trust herself anywhere near a half-naked Theo. Which was a galling admission to make, but true… As for the rest, she had brought a skirt and three summer dresses, plus, mindful of the inclement nature of the British weather, a pair of jeans and a sweater.

June in Greece was a lot hotter than it was at home, and this house and its inhabitants were a lot more elegant than the little hotel she had intended staying in, she thought dryly.

Taking one of the dresses from the hanger, she slipped it on. It was Indian cotton dyed in a swirling pattern of blues and greens, sleeveless with a low square neck. It had a pin-tucked bodice and a long flowing skirt that ended mid-calf. It was a style she favoured—easy wash, easy wear—and not very expensive. She crossed to the dressing table and sat down, and for a brief moment she felt like putting her head in her hands and having a good cry.

She did not fit in in this house or in this lifestyle of great wealth and private jets. But she had a growing conviction her beloved Stephen would very quickly adapt, and where would that leave her then? Married to Theo if he had his way. It didn't bear thinking about.

So instead she followed her familiar pattern and tried to ignore the problem. She plucked her hairbrush from her toilet bag, and swept her hair back and secured it at the nape of her neck with a multicoloured enamelled slide. An application of moisturiser to her pale face and she was ready. She slipped her feet into a pair of flat tan leather sandals, and left the bedroom.

The house was silent and dim behind the closed shutters of the landing and stairs, but there was no mistaking the opulence of the place. A magnificent marble staircase was the centre feature, leading down to a huge circular hall with an exquisite mosaic-tiled floor depicting an ancient Greek myth. Elegant marble columns flanked four huge double doors and Willow paused for a moment, not sure which way to go. The sound of voices led her towards a partially open door, and, walking through, she found herself in a large but surprisingly comfortable-looking room.

A huge colourful rug complemented a ceramic-tiled floor. Big squashy sofas were set around a fireplace at one end, and possibly the biggest television set she had ever seen filled another corner. A few assorted chairs, occasional tables, a desk, and a heavy wood cabinet holding an array of drinks made up the rest of the furnishings.

'We thought you had got lost.' Theo's deep, dark drawl had her head turning towards the huge glass doors that opened out onto the terrace.

'I wish I could,' she muttered. He was standing three feet away, but at least he had put some shorts on, she noted, her mouth running dry. With the light behind him his huge black shadow seemed to be reaching out to swallow her whole, and inexplicably she shivered.

'You don't mean that, Willow. You would hate to be parted from our son.' He stepped towards her. 'From what I have seen he is a happy, well-balanced little boy and he adores you. As for you and I—our marriage can be as good as you want to make it.' He looked at her with amusement and something more in his black eyes. 'We both know the sex is great, which is a very good place to start.'

'Is that all you ever think about?' Willow shot back. 'I have a job, a home and a life I love and for the umpteenth time I am not going to marry you, Theo. Stephen and I are here for a week's holiday, full stop.'

'You can write anywhere in the world, Willow, and I am not an ogre—you can keep your home. It will make a nice holiday cottage, but that is all. Anything else you need I will provide.'

'I don't need anyone to provide for me,' she snapped. He was like a juggernaut ignoring every refusal she put in his path, and blithely carrying on. 'I can do that on my own.'

He cast her a slow assessing look. 'I know,' he agreed. 'Stephen is a credit to you, and you have proved your ability to succeed in life to the whole world, but it must have been hard work. Now it is time for you to relinquish the reins a little, relax, and, how do you say it? Smell the roses.' His firm lips quirked at the corners and he smiled down at her. 'Stop creating problems where there are none, Willow. Now I have to dress, but my mother is waiting to meet you again, and don't worry—she is so entranced with Stephanos that all is forgiven.'

Stephanos. It was happening already, the Kadros take-over of her son, Willow thought, fear and anger making her voice sharp. 'His name is Stephen, and I have nothing to be forgiven for,' she said determinedly, straightening her shoulders. 'However, you could take a look at your own behaviour.' She attempted to walk past him, but steely fingers closed around her arm.

She tried to wrench free, but in a heartbeat she was spun around and enfolded in a tight embrace. The shock of being pressed against his bare chest, all sleek, rippling muscle, made her gasp. 'Let me go.'

'We have an audience, so be quiet and listen.' Theo stared down into her face, his own hard. 'Your one saving grace is that you named our son Stephen; my father's name was Stephanos. My mother is a religious woman and she is a great believer in fate. She is convinced your naming our son Stephen was God's will and therefore she forgives you for not making him known to us sooner. But understand this,' he commanded with icy force, 'I am nowhere near as forgiving as my mother and if you do anything at all to upset her I will make you wish you were never born.'

'As if I would,' Willow said with a negative shake of her dark head. This man did not know her at all. But even as he threatened her she was intensely aware of the clean, male scent of him, and she felt her breasts hardening at the close contact with his massive chest. Tensing, she raised her hands between their two bodies in the hope of pushing him away. 'And for your information Stephen was named after the ambulance driver who delivered him,' she told him bluntly.

His dark head suddenly jerked back and his hold on her loosened as he stared down at her with incredulous black eyes. 'An ambulance driver—what on earth for?'

Willow took the chance to escape, and stepped back quickly. 'Figure it out for yourself. You're so smart.'

'Wait a minute.' She was hauled back by a strong arm snaking around her waist, and the chill in Theo's dark eyes was now pronounced. 'Was he a lover?'

The total incongruity of his question made her laugh out loud. 'Hardly.' She lifted sparkling blue eyes to his. 'In fact, I might have put the poor young man off sex for life. It was his first week in the job when I called for an ambulance because the birth was imminent. Unfortunately by the time the ambulance arrived it was too late. Stephen had to deliver my baby in the bedroom.'

Theo's arm fell from her waist and he stared down at her in shock. 'A man...? A complete stranger...?' He shook his dark head incredulously.

Willow grinned; she had succeeded in leaving him speechless. Spinning around, she walked along the terrace to where a circular table was set for breakfast under the shade of a huge parasol. Mrs Kadros was already there, sitting next to Stephen, a beaming smile on her face.

'Ah, Willow, good morning. Please sit down. You have no idea how happy you have made me.'

'Good morning, Mrs Kadros,' she said rather nervously.

'Oh, no, dear, please, you must call me Judy. And I shall call you Willow. I was born and brought up in America so we don't stand on ceremony here. Though sometimes my beloved Stephanos used to despair of my open ways, but I always found ways to reassure him,' she said with a slightly naughty chuckle.

'Then good morning again, Judy.' Willow grinned. There was something infectious about the older woman's humour, and her first name was refreshingly more American than Greek. Pulling out a chair, Willow sat down on the opposite side of her son. 'I must thank you for having Stephen and I stay for a short holiday.' She felt better having clarified the situation with Judy. Willow was not going to marry her son, whatever Theo thought.

'My pleasure.' Judy smiled and leaned over and filled the coffee-cup at Willow's place setting. She then beckoned to the young Greek maid standing a few feet away, and said in an aside, 'Fresh coffee, please, Marta,' and, grinning back at Willow, she asked, 'Now, what would you like to eat? Just name it and Marta will prepare it for you.'

'Coffee and a roll will be fine. I never eat much breakfast,' Willow said truthfully.

'You will here, Mum—the food is great,' Stephen cut in, glancing up at her and talking with his mouth half full. 'You must try these pastry things with honey on them. They are much better than porridge.'

Willow grimaced. 'Not so good for your teeth, though; make sure you clean them after you have finished eating.' Pouring some cream in her coffee, she lifted the cup to her lips; she needed this.

'You are perfectly right,' Judy supported her. 'But excuse an old woman for spoiling the little one.'

'I'm not little,' Stephen said smartly. 'I am eight.'

'Sorry, Stephanos, of course you are a big boy, and I have no doubt you will end up as tall as your father in time.'

'Will I really, Mum?' he asked.

'I think it is a pretty safe bet,' Willow said dryly, grinning down into his beloved face. He was still young enough to turn to her for confirmation, his trust in her still absolute. But for how much longer, she wondered, now that his father was on the scene?

'I can see I am going to end up feeling like the midget of the family very soon,' Judy joked, and, turning to Willow, she added, 'But I don't care, set against the joy of seeing my grandson grow up. You cannot imagine how marvellous it is to have Theo's child in my house, my grandson. His grandfather must be rejoicing in heaven, I am sure,' and to Willow's surprise moisture glazed Judy's golden brown eyes. 'Forgive me, I am still a little emotional.'

'No, please, there is nothing to forgive.' Then, taking the bull by the horn, she did what she knew she had to do. 'If anyone needs forgiveness it is me. I should have tried to get in touch with you sooner.' There, she had said it. Willow took a deep, steadying breath and lifted the cup of coffee to her lips and drained the contents in one go.

'Go and find your father, Stephanos, and tell him to dress you properly before coming back or you will burn.'

'Oh, I'll do that.' Willow made to rise. 'I forgot too much exposure to the sun is so harmful.' Judy must think she was the world's worst mother.

'No.' Judy laid a restraining hand on her arm as Willow went to follow Stephen's quick departure from the table.

'No, stay. Let Theo learn a little of what is involved in looking after a child. Plus, I want to talk to you.'

Willow settled back in the chair, her blue eyes wary. Here it came—question-and-answer time; she was not looking forward to it one bit.

'There is no need to look so fearful, dear. Theo has told me everything.' Not everything, surely, Willow thought, turning scarlet with embarrassment. 'And you have nothing to be ashamed of. He told me how you went looking for him in London when you knew you were pregnant, and how the house he and Anna had shared was in the process of being converted to offices. He also said that he had never given you his home address or even a telephone number,' she said, disapproval evident in her tone.

'I love my son, Willow, but I am not blind to his faults. I know that when he was in his twenties he had many women, with no thought of commitment. If anyone was at fault it was Theo. He had no right to seduce you and then marry another woman only six months later, and you pregnant with his child. No girl should have to suffer such indignity, and you took the only course of action open to you. I would have done the same myself in your position. So let us say no more about it; the matter is closed.'

'That is very generous of you,' Willow said softly. Her blue eyes met with Judy's shimmering brown and there was no doubting the sincerity in the older woman's compassionate gaze. 'But I doubt if Theo thinks the same way.'

'Someone taking my name in vain?'

Willow jerked upright in her seat at the sound of Theo's deep drawl. He came to a stop a foot away, and she felt the hairs on the back of her neck prickle in instant awareness. Reluctantly she turned her head to look up at him. He was dressed in a casually cut linen suit and a white open-necked shirt and he was pulling out the chair next to hers.

'So?' he prompted with a brief smile for her and a brilliant one for his mother as he sat down. Stephen, now dressed in khaki shorts and a crisp white tee shirt, had been following along behind his father and quickly scrambled back into his seat.

'What does in vain mean, Mum?' Stephen asked, grabbing her attention.

'It usually means,' Judy responded, with her gaze narrowed on Theo, rather than Stephen, 'that when you listen in to other people's conversation and hear your name mentioned, invariably the people concerned are not speaking well of you.'

Willow turned puzzled eyes back to Theo, and to her utter amazement she watched as a dull tide of red swept along his high cheekbones. He was actually embarrassed. That had to be another first…

'I was just reassuring Willow that I don't hold her responsible for keeping me apart from my grandson. She must have been very young and very frightened.'

'Mum was eighteen when she had me,' Stephen cut in, and for once Willow wished he were not quite so bright or so inquisitive.

'Eighteen?' Judy gasped and the look she gave her son could have stripped paint. 'Oh, you poor child,' she said, her sympathetic gaze settling on Willow. 'But no doubt your family helped you?' she prompted.

'We don't have any family. My grandmother and my great-grandmother both died the year before I was born,' Stephen continued. 'We live in Great-grandma's house now and we have tons of photographs of them and things.'

It was getting worse by the second. 'Really, Stephen, I don't think anyone is interested,' Willow admonished.

'Yes, do go on, son,' Theo encouraged him, his attention suddenly fully arrested.

'Well, Tess, our neighbour, knew them both; in fact everyone in the village knew them. Isn't that right, Mum?'

'Yes.' What else could she say?

'It is sad to lose one's grandmother, but to lose your mother at the same time must have been devastating. Was it an accident?' Judy asked quietly.

'No, well, yes. Half and half,' Willow said, clenching her hands tightly on her lap. She wished everyone would drop the subject.

'Half and half is no answer,' Theo opined flatly and, flicking him a sidelong glance, she saw the distaste in his dark eyes.

What had she expected from the man—sympathy, compassion or at the very least some tact? She must be mad; the man hadn't a grain of sensitivity in his soul.

'You're right, Theo, of course.' She smiled thinly. 'My grandmother died of natural causes at Easter time and if you remember I visited my mother in India the same summer.' The bitterness in her blue eyes was only for him. To the other two at the table she was still smiling. 'Mum got caught up in a riot in India, the week before she was due to come home in the September, and she was killed by a stray bullet.'

'I'm sorry,' Theo murmured.

She tore her gaze away from his. Too little, too late, she thought scathingly, and she did not see the colour drain from his face or the shock in his dark eyes.

'Oh, you poor girl,' Judy murmured.

'Yes, well, it was a long time ago, and Stephen and I manage very well on our own.' She reached out and touched her son's arm, more for her own comfort than his.

Then to her amazement Judy directed what sounded like a tirade in Greek at Theo.

'Forgive my lapse in manners.' Judy finally resumed speaking in English. 'But you understand, Willow, you are a mother yourself—sometimes a son needs to be lectured, whatever their age.' With a lingering glance at Theo's stony face, she smiled at Stephen and added, 'Now, young man, how would you like to visit the biggest toy shop in Athens?'

'Not so fast, Mother,' Theo said firmly. 'Stephen.' He turned his dark gaze on the boy, and at the same time he curved his arm around Willow's shoulder. His touch caused a jolt of awareness through her slender body but what followed left her speechless.

'If you agree, Stephen, you and your mum will never have to manage on your own again.' He was throwing her own words back in her face, Willow thought incredulously. 'You see, your mother and I want to get married, as soon as possible, so we can all live together as one happy family.'

'Really?' Stephen questioned. 'We will be just like a proper family.'

Willow tried to jerk away from Theo's hold, but his long brown fingers merely shifted to curve around the nape of her neck. His dark head bent towards her. 'Isn't that right, darling?'

Stephen was incandescent with joy. It was his dream come true, and, leaping out of his chair, he flung his arms around Willow's waist. She looked down into her son's eyes, and saw the hope and longing there. With a sinking heart she realised that, while she had no trouble at all in refusing Theo's proposal of marriage, she could not bear to disappoint Stephen. She was left with no choice.

'Yes, Theo.' She bared her teeth in a smile, her blue eyes

fastening on him, cold fear and fury in the sapphire depths. The ruthless devil had done it again, used her son and emotional blackmail to get exactly what he wanted. Well, he might think he had forced her into marriage, but if he thought for one second she was going to play the obedient little wife, he was in for a rude awakening. 'Eventually,' she qualified.

But her 'eventually,' was drowned out by Judy's shouting. Marta and Takis appeared with glasses and a bottle of champagne, and Judy proposed a toast to long life and happiness. Willow smiled and pretended she was happy, but inside she was fuming, her mind racing to find a way out of her dilemma.

But the biggest problem was Stephen. One glance at his beaming face and there was no mistaking his sheer delight at the thought of having his mother and father together, in his own words, *a proper family...*

CHAPTER NINE

'No,' WILLOW said, and stopped in the middle of the plush boutique. 'I am not trying on another thing,' she stated emphatically. She was hot, she was sweaty, and she was fed up.

Theo had driven them all into Athens. At Judy's suggestion it had been arranged that she would take Stephen to look for toys and to buy a wedding present for his mum and dad. Stephen had quite happily gone off with his grandmother and Willow had been left with Theo with Judy's last instruction ringing in her ears. 'Take her shopping, Theo, and make sure she has something fabulous to wear; I feel a party coming on.'

Willow glanced across at him. He was lounging on a velvet sofa looking perfectly relaxed. Obviously he was used to buying women clothes, she thought dryly. Even the sales lady was drooling over him as he instructed her on what garments his fiancée should try with all the arrogance of some Eastern potentate decorating his favourite choice from his harem.

Willow felt like a clothes hanger, and the last gown he had picked was the final straw. She had had enough. Elegant suits, designer casuals, three evening gowns—she was sick to death of taking her clothes on and off, and she had nó intention of buying any of them.

Marching over to where Theo sat, she frowned angrily down at him. 'I don't know about you, but I am leaving,' she snapped. 'And I am not buying anything here—they are over-priced and pretty useless. So, if you want some woman to try on that green slip—' she gestured wildly with her hand to the slither of silk that the assistant was holding '—then ask her, I am sure she will oblige for you,' she said snidely.

Leaping to his feet, Theo smiled and said something in Greek to the sales lady. Gripping Willow's arm, he swung her around to face him, his back to the rest of the shop.

'As my wife you have a position to uphold,' he stated, his cool gaze narrowing on her flushed and furious face. 'And beautiful though you are, Willow, your dress sense leaves a lot to be desired. Didn't you know the hippy look went out over forty years ago?' he prompted sarcastically.

For some inexplicable reason his words hurt, and she fought hard not to let her feelings show. 'Maybe that is true in your world of designer clothes and the latest fashion fad, but not in mine,' she said flatly. 'Cheap and cheerful is much more practical.' She stiffened her shoulders, her blue eyes boldly meeting his. He was an insensitive jerk; why should she care about a word he said? 'And once more I am not going to marry you!' she said defiantly.

Theo's jaw clenched. He saw the flicker of hurt in her expressive eyes and he felt like the world's worst heel. Willow was a proud, capable woman who had made a success of her life with no help from anyone, and certainly not him. She had given birth to his son when she was still a teenager with only a stranger to help her. All this while still grieving for her mother and grandmother at the same time, as he had learned to his horror this morning. A guilty conscience had turned his stomach and torn at his heart ever since. Even his own mother had lashed into him when she had found out, and he didn't blame her.

He was a man who had never wanted for anything of monetary value in his life, but he was sure Willow had not had the same advantage eight years ago and he was the only one to blame.

'Okay, leave the green,' he instructed. 'But you are taking the rest; I insist. And unless you want to tell Stephen that you lied this morning and therefore break his heart, you will marry me on Thursday.'

His eyes narrowed on her face, his tone determined. She felt his fingers flexing on her arm, and she didn't want to feel anything. Her eyes lifted to his, the silence between them charged. Willow could feel it in every nerve in her body, a curious pulsing awareness; it was the ultimate moment of truth. Could she break her son's heart, or risk her own?

She swallowed hard, her black lashes flickering down to hide the expression in her eyes. There was only one answer she could give him... 'Yes, Thursday it is,' she said finally, resigned to the inevitable.

'Good.' His face immediately altered, his eyes smiling down at her. 'I knew you would eventually see sense,' and he let go of her to pay for the purchases.

If he wanted to waste his money, let him. It was all he had to give a woman anyway, Willow thought bitterly, and walked out into the sunlight. That and great sex, an imp of devilment whispered in her brain just as a strong hand closed around her arm and stopped her in her tracks...

'I have had just about as much as I can take for one day,' Theo snarled. 'I am sorry if I upset you, but don't you ever walk out on me again.'

'Upset? I'm not upset.' Her finely arched brows rose in query. 'Why would I be? After all, it is not every day a girl gets relocated to the lap of luxury in Greece, showered in designer clothes and gets a rich husband thrown in,' she said with biting sarcasm.

'Well, I damn well am.' Theo swore, losing his superb

control. Spinning her around, he trapped her against the building with his hands on the wall either side of her head. 'If you want to make me feel guilty, then consider it done. How the hell did you think I felt this morning when I discovered, not only had I got you pregnant, but that an ambulance driver delivered our son? And, worse still, that you were totally on your own, having lost both your mother and your grandmother. I was disgusted.'

'So I noticed,' Willow cut in bitterly.

'Not with you, with myself,' Theo declared adamantly. 'My own mother was ashamed of me when she discovered how young and alone you were and tore into me as she has never done since I was a child.'

'I did wonder why she was yelling at you. Why didn't you just tell her the truth? It was only a one-night stand and after I left you,' Willow snapped back.

'I would never discredit the mother of my son in such a way,' he said between gritted teeth. 'And you were never just a one-night stand to me, whatever you may think. I asked you to stay with me, remember.'

'You said so the other night,' she reminded him bluntly.

'*Theos!* Must you question every damn thing I say?' Theo struggled to retain his temper. 'I can't do right for doing wrong where you are concerned. The only reason I bought you a few clothes was because I thought you might enjoy them and because it was the least I could do.' He had thought she would be delighted with a new wardrobe of clothes; every other woman he had ever known would have been all over him like a rash. But Willow was not like any other woman. Now his action just seemed crass, a sop to his conscience, and an insult to Willow.

Wide-eyed, she stared up at him, shocked by his outburst, and stunned that he had actually admitted to feelings of guilt. Then she gave a little mocking laugh. 'Thanks, I think.'

His eyes became bleak with bitterness. 'With hindsight I should have tried harder to keep in touch with you, but you lied to me and didn't give me the opportunity. When you knew you were pregnant with my child, one trip to an old address was not much of a search.'

It was all her fault again... She might have guessed his guilty feelings would not last long, and they had almost taken her in.

'I made more than one attempt,' she said, her own temper rising. 'Seven months pregnant, I boarded the train for London with the address of your London office in my pocket. In the magazine I bought to read on the journey were the pictures of your wedding to Dianne. I got off at the next stop and went home. Is that good enough for you?' She wanted the swine to feel guilty; it was the only way she could lash out at him. He had blocked all her other avenues of escape. 'Or maybe I should have followed you on your honeymoon,' she gibed.

For an interminable moment Theo just stood there regarding her in total silence, his face an inscrutable mask. 'No, and I am sorry you had to find out that way,' he finally said quietly. 'Obviously talking about the past is a futile exercise. It is the future we have to look forward to.' With a quick dip of his dark head, his mouth covered hers and he kissed her. She couldn't believe it, but a long moment later when he raised his head and allowed her to breathe again she was too shaken to care.

How did he do that? she asked herself again. He managed to reduce her to a quivering mass of jelly with one kiss. And in the middle of the day on a crowded pavement where the world and his wife could watch, she realised with dawning embarrassment. Lifting her eyes, she stared up into his darkly handsome face. 'What was that for?' she asked dazedly.

'To shut you up,' he said with a wry smile. 'You infuriating madam. I have not argued in the street since I was a schoolboy, and I've had enough guilt for one day. I am declaring a truce.' And tucking her arm in his, he set off along the street.

Five minutes later, when Theo stopped outside a very elegant black door with the name in gold lettering, she pulled her hand from his arm. 'Oh, no! Not more shopping.'

He slid an arm around her shoulder and a slow smile curved his wide, sensual mouth as she looked stubbornly up at him. 'Humour me, Willow. Last stop, I promise, and then we can meet the others for lunch.'

A moment later as Theo ushered her through the door, and into the shop, it was with a grim lack of humour that she looked around and saw it was a jeweller's.

'As my fiancée you must wear my ring.' She opened her mouth to object but he pressed a finger over her lips. 'And don't argue—truce, remember?'

So far he had got all his own way. His finger was still on her mouth and, unless she could get over this terrible disability of losing her mind whenever he touched her, he was likely to continue doing so.

But she got her revenge when it came to choosing the ring. Forced into agreeing to marry him, and still smarting from his crack about her dress sense, she picked the biggest platinum-mounted solitaire blue diamond the jeweller could provide. To add to the ostentatious engagement ring she chose an equally ostentatious diamond-studded platinum wedding band.

Theo gave her a curious look. 'Are you sure they are what you want?'

'Certainly.' She tilted her head to look up at him, a patently false smile twisting her luscious lips. 'As the wife of a filthy rich man, you said I have to look the part. And I just love them,' she gushed, 'darling.' She thought he would be furious but to her astonishment his lips curved in an achingly familiar crooked smile.

'*Touché,* darling,' he drawled with rueful amusement, and bought the rings.

Two days later Stephen sat on her bed and watched her dress. 'I wish I was going to the party.'

'When you are a bit older, but tonight you have to be a good boy for Marta and do as she says. Right?'

'Right,' he agreed.

Willow grinned down at her son. 'Well, what do you think, Stephen? Will I do?' And with a shaky hand she smoothed down the strapless, long slim-fitting sheath of wild blue silk she had chosen from the clothes Theo had insisted on buying for her. She had pinned her long black hair on top of her head, and the severity of the style emphasised the perfect outline of her face and the white swan-like elegance of her neck. Her make-up was light as usual: moisturiser, lip gloss and a touch of mascara. On her feet she wore high-heeled sandals that matched the dress perfectly. She had painted her nails a light pink and she had never felt so dressed up in her life, or so nervous.

'You look beautiful, Mum.'

'And I second that,' Theo said.

She hadn't heard him enter, and she lifted anxious dark eyes to his. The full impact of him attired in sophisticated dinner clothes sent every one of her senses haywire.

His hooded gaze roamed over her with studied masculine appraisal, and the eyes he lifted to hers were glittering with a hot possessiveness that she could not fail to recognise. It hit her with the force of a lightning bolt. She had agreed to marry this man, and tonight was their engagement party. She must be crazy, and as he walked towards her she felt panic rising inside her. 'Is it time to go?'

His firm lips curved in a slow, sexy smile. 'Some might say well past time, given we have a son,' he drawled, and took her trembling hand in his. Turning to Stephen, he added, 'Run along to your room. Marta is waiting, and she has a surprise for you.'

Stephen held his little face up for Willow's goodnight kiss with some impatience and then darted from the room.

'Ready?' Theo looked down into her blue eyes, and she nodded, too nervous to speak.

The party had been Judy's idea, and she had made no secret of the fact that she had an eight-year-old grandson called Stephanos. Her joy was unrestrained. But as Willow stood by Theo's side to greet the guests she could almost feel the shock waves when he introduced her as his fiancée. She twisted the huge diamond ring nervously around her finger, and wished she had never chosen it. Her joke had spectacularly backfired, as guest after female guest demanded to see it, and was apparently awed by its magnificence, but she could sense their insincerity.

She told herself she didn't care about other people's reaction, but it was hard when she had to suffer a few barbed comments about how wonderful it must be for her and her son to find Theo again, and how they would now never have to want for anything. They might as well have come out and said 'gold-digger'. The huge diamond ring did not help her cause one bit.

'Nice friends you have,' she murmured with a sarcastic lift of one finely arched brow in Theo's direction. 'But if you will excuse me I think I need a drink.'

He shrugged lightly, emphasising the width of his broad shoulders underneath the elegant dinner suit. 'What did you expect?' he said with a cynical curve to his expressive mouth. 'Introducing a fiancée and a son in one evening was bound to cause gossip, and whose fault is that?' There was something in his voice that sent a sudden unease sliding through her. 'You surely didn't expect me to hide you both away, darling. That was always your solution, but not mine, I will not allow it.'

Sliding a casual arm around her waist, he pulled her into his side. 'Don't look so tense; you're an incredibly beautiful woman.' He scanned her exquisite features with glittering dark eyes. 'More so than any woman here. Relax and enjoy the party.' And he lifted her hand and raised it to his lips, pressing a lingering kiss against her knuckles. His dark gaze held hers with a compelling intensity. 'As for the ring, the jeweller informed me when I paid for it that I was an extremely lucky man. You are one of the few women in the world with hands elegant enough and fingers long enough to wear it. These women here tonight are just green with envy, believe me.' Strangely she did as he added, 'Fortunately our marriage will be a nine-day wonder, if that, and then you and I can get on with our lives…together.'

Theo complimenting her, and reassuring her—that had to be a first. There was something in his tone that made her pulse race, and yet his arm around her waist gave her the oddest feeling of being protected and at peace with the world. It was a lethal combination and it worried her slightly. Swiftly lowering her gaze, she freed her hand from his, frightened that he would notice, and tried to slip from his restraining arm.

'Wowee, Theo! No wonder you want to hang onto her,' a deeply accented male voice said with a laugh, noting her struggle. 'She is perfection; you must introduce me.'

Willow stilled in the curve of Theo's arm. She had been in serious danger of making a fool of herself in front of all the guests and this person in particular. She glanced at the man and her eyes widened appreciatively. Theo apart, he had to be the best-looking man at the party. Maybe an inch taller than her, and two or three years older, he had long black curly hair tied back with a leather thong in a ponytail. His dinner suit was a flamboyant rich blue, and yet it suited him, and the gleaming golden eyes smiling into hers were full of fun.

'Leo, I am surprised you could make it,' Theo said with a coolness that sent shivers down Willow's spine.

'You know me, Theo—I can't resist a party.' He smiled at Willow. 'I think your fiancé is reluctant to tell me your name, beautiful lady. He is probably afraid of the competition.' He grinned wickedly. '*Moi*—' he lifted his hand to his heart '—your slave for life,' and he winked.

Willow laughed out loud. He was outrageous, but a welcome relief from the stiff formality of the rest of the guests.

'That's enough, Leo,' Theo said grimly. Willow felt the tightening of Theo's arm around her waist and the sudden tension in every muscle in his body beneath the immaculate dinner suit, and she looked at the other man with interest. A man that could get a reaction from the intimidating Theo Kadros had to be a rarity.

'My fiancée Willow, and she is out of bounds to you.'

'Why, Theo?' she said sweetly, beginning to hugely enjoy herself. 'Surely you can't be jealous? Leo was only being polite.'

Theo spared her a dark glance. 'Maybe, but now it is time we mingled,' and, ignoring the other man, he urged her towards another group of people.

'What have you got against Leo?' she asked.

'Nothing at all. He is a good friend. I have known him for years. But he is also a notorious womaniser. For some reason women adore him, and I am taking no chances.'

Surprised, Willow glanced up at him and was stunned to see he was serious. Talk about the pot calling the kettle black, she thought dryly.

The buffet was announced, and Judy joined them as they made their way to the large dining room. Anna and her husband appeared and for the next hour they ate and drank together, with frequent exclamations by Anna: 'I still can't believe it. You, of all people, Willow!'

Willow had met Anna and her two daughters yesterday when they had arrived at the house eager to meet the new addition to the family. Stephen had been an instant hit with the two girls, but Anna had been in a state of shock. She'd spent the morning giving her brother disapproving looks, until he had escaped to his office to put in a few hours' work. Then she had taken Willow out for lunch and a girlie afternoon in Athens, and spent most of the time apologising to her. She'd stated that he must have loved Willow all along.

Theo was leaning against the wall at the party, watching his mother and sister, their faces animated as they ate and drank and gossiped. But his eyes narrowed on Willow as he caught sight of the flicker of strain in her expressive blue eyes, even as her carefully composed features creased into a smile.

These three women were his family and it hit him forcibly that he felt the same protective instinct for Willow as he did for the other two women in his life. And inexplicably he felt angry with his guests for not immediately seeing Willow as he did.

She was an exceptional woman in a hundred different ways. Proud, independent and a wonderful mother, not to mention the most exquisitely beautiful female he had ever seen. Yet there was no vanity about her; she seemed totally unaware of her own power. There wasn't a man in this room who would not leap at the chance to be in his shoes, and she had been right before. He was jealous.

'If you're finished eating, Willow, perhaps you would like a breath of fresh air?'

Willow lifted her head and met his dark gaze almost with relief. It was hot inside and the noise was making her head ache, not to mention her feeling the censure of all eyes. 'You read my mind,' she said with unaccustomed flippancy, and took the hand he held out to help her to her feet.

Theo led her out onto the terrace, deftly fielding the many salutations from his friends as they passed. She drew in a lungful of the cool night air, a soft sigh escaping her.

'Better?' Theo asked quietly.

'Yes,' Willow murmured. Their hands still linked together, she smiled briefly up at him.

'Good.' Theo stopped and looked down at her, his expression oddly serious. 'This party…' He gestured with his free hand to the brilliantly lit rooms and the crowd of people spilling out onto the terrace. 'You don't need to worry— these people will very quickly accept your sudden appearance in my life. Any who don't will have me to deal with, I promise you.'

She lifted smiling eyes to his. Even when he was trying to be serious his inbuilt arrogance very quickly surfaced, she thought with wry amusement. 'From kidnapper to white knight in four days, Theo,' she quipped with a chuckle. 'That is some going, even for you, but amazingly I think I believe you. None of this lot would dare argue with you.'

The hand holding hers slid around her waist and he drew her closer. 'So I amuse you, do I?' His dark eyes lit with laughter and a deepening sexual gleam that promised retribution of the most basic kind. 'You would dare laugh at me,' he drawled huskily, and his dark head lowered, his warm breath brushing her cheek, 'when all I am trying to do…'

'I know very well what you are trying to do,' she responded with a sharp intake of breath, and her whole body trembled as his grip tightened around her waist. He was going to kiss her, she knew it, and she swayed towards him.

'Willow Blain, that's it!' A very English voice broke the simmering sexual tension between them. 'I have been racking my brains all evening, trying to remember where I had seen you before. I never forget a face, and then it suddenly struck me.'

Theo's head jerked up and he looked at the fair-haired Englishman, standing not two paces away, grinning at Willow like a Cheshire cat, and he suddenly wished he could strike him again, in the physical sense. Instead he steadied Willow, withdrew his hand from hers and took a step aside. 'Charles, nice to see you,' he said blandly. 'Enjoying the party, I hope.'

'I am now,' he said, not taking his eyes from Willow. 'It is you, isn't it? Your picture was in a British tabloid last week; we get them all at the embassy. J. W. Paxton the crime writer revealed as a woman. I am right, aren't I? And to think I have read all his books and never guessed, I mean your books—they are brilliant,' he ended, blushing.

With ingrained politeness Willow acknowledged the fair, lanky man's compliments, and discovered he was First Secretary to the British Ambassador in Athens. He finally left only after Willow promised to give him a signed copy of her latest book.

'Another conquest, I see,' Theo remarked as Charles vanished back inside. 'And no doubt within minutes everyone will know who you are. Do you want to go back inside and face your public?' he asked noncommittally.

'Hardly my public. My first book only came out in Greek a month or so ago so no one will know me.'

'Believe me they will once Charles has spread the news. If there is one thing that appeals more than money to a Greek, it is the Arts, and specifically the perceived intellectual pursuits like writing.'

'Well, you are Greek so I bow to your superior judgement,' she conceded and half turned to face him. 'But if you don't mind I won't go back inside. I have had enough of people for one evening.'

His hand closed around her bare arm. 'Then come with me.' She wasn't prepared when he bent his head and kissed her firmly but sweetly.

He had not touched her in a sexual way in two days. Willow had decided in her own head it was because he had already got her agreement to marry him and he was no longer interested. But now, reeling from the unexpected warmth of his kiss, she wondered if she was wrong, and unthinkingly followed him down the steps into the garden. Five minutes later she was standing in a small circular patio surrounded with sweet-scented blossoming shrubs with the sound of water tinkling over the centrepiece of the fountain that occupied the middle.

'It is like a secret garden.' She grinned, spinning around. 'Quite magical and beautiful.'

'So are you,' Theo murmured in a deep, husky drawl. 'Unbelievably so.'

Willow stilled, his unexpected compliment taking her breath away. She looked at him standing in a patch of golden light created by strategically placed lamps, and he looked so good she could not take her eyes off him. Tall, dark and handsome did not do him justice. He was a feast of all the senses. The sound of his voice, the masculine scent of him. The taste and strength of him, and every magnificent inch of his six-foot-four frame, naked or clothed, delighted her eye. She felt her breasts harden and swell, and her tongue flicked out to lick her suddenly dry lips. She needed him in the most wanton, basic way, and her blue eyes widened in shock at the realisation.

'Willow. What is it?' He stepped forward, his gleaming dark eyes fixed on her. The air between them was heavy with sexual tension.

She shook her head and strands of her silken hair were flying free from the precariously placed pins to fall in soft rippling waves around her face. She didn't recognise the purely sensual being she appeared to become whenever she was alone with Theo, and she wasn't sure she liked it. It smacked of weakness, but she was utterly helpless to deny her feelings. 'Nothing…' she murmured unsteadily.

But there was nothing unsteady about the arms that reached out and enfolded her or the way he kissed her. She wound her arms around his neck at the first taste of his tongue on hers and her legs went weak.

He broke the kiss and she groaned and then sighed her pleasure as she felt the hot warmth of his mouth trail down her throat. With a primitive growl he pulled down the front of her dress and found her breasts. His tongue flicked the engorged nipples and her back arched in a curve of incredible excitement.

She raked one hand through his hair and the other reached for the buttons of his shirt. She tore one free and slipped her hand beneath the silk, and let her palm stroke up over the hard wall of his chest. She could feel the thundering beat of his heart beneath her palm, and she rejoiced in the discovery that he was as helpless as her to control the wild, wonderful urge that kept them locked together. But she was wrong…

His dark head lifted. 'You have the most amazingly sensitive breasts,' he breathed, his smouldering eyes gleaming down into hers as he adjusted her gown, 'but here is not the place.' And he brushed her hand from his chest.

Willow stared at him in shock, every nerve in her body vibrating with raw sensation, and then shame hit her. He had led her on deliberately.

'No, no, Willow.' As if reading her mind, he swiftly denied her assumption, and enfolded her into his arms, holding her firmly against him. 'Anyone might find us here,' he murmured against her ear. 'That is all I meant.' And with his strong hands stroking soothingly up and down her spine Willow began to relax. 'Believe me, this is as hard for me as it is for you.' He slowly eased her away from him, and, resting his hands on her shoulders, he added, 'More so for me,' and he smiled ruefully down into her flushed face. 'But we are getting married on Thursday, and even if I have to spend the next three days in a cold shower, I am determined to do it right this time and we are going to wait until our wedding night.'

CHAPTER TEN

THEY were married in a civil ceremony three days later in the garden of Judy's home. To Willow's amazement Tess and her husband Bob appeared, as did Stephen's young friend Tommy, courtesy of Theo's private jet.

In a strapless cream satin dress that moulded her figure to perfection and with her hair swept off her face by two diamond clips, a wedding gift from Theo, Willow stood like a tall, beautiful statue posing for photographs with her new husband in the hot summer sun.

The professional photographer called to them, 'Okay, one more, with all the family, and that should be enough to show the grandchildren.' With his use of the plural Willow wondered anxiously what would happen if she did become pregnant again. On her lunch date with Anna a couple of days ago, the talk had got around to children, and with Anna's help Willow had visited her doctor. A simple test had confirmed that she was not already pregnant and she was now equipped with the pill. The first month was not guaranteed but hopefully it would never happen.

Still, with luck she would be okay, she thought, worriedly chewing her bottom lip. Much as she would love another child, she dared not take the risk. This marriage was for eight years only, not a commitment for life, she constantly reminded herself. She saw no reason to tell Theo of her precautions. He had taken over her life almost completely, but in the most personal areas of her life she was determined to retain control, and she slanted a wary glance up at her husband.

Theo caught her worried gaze. 'Stop it, Willow, it might never happen.' He gathered her into his arms and kissed her full on the mouth with a deep, drugging tenderness that drove every thought from her head. Only Stephen pulling on his jacket finally forced him to release her.

'Hey, Dad, that's mushy,' Stephen said indignantly, and everyone laughed.

The champagne flowed freely and the running buffet was a gourmet's delight. Willow lost track of the people who congratulated them; all she was aware of was Theo's tall, commanding presence close to her side through countless toasts and teasing. A quartet started to play and with great ceremony Theo led her out onto the terrace and took her in his arms.

'Have I told you today, Mrs Kadros—' his dark eyes captured hers, a gleam of triumph and something else in the inky depths that made her heart squeeze in her chest '—my wife—' he savoured the two words as he held her closer and she had no choice but to lift her hands to his broad shoulders as they moved slowly around to the music '—you look stunningly beautiful, and absolutely divine?' Bodies touching shoulder to thigh, legs entwined as he spun her around, Willow almost believed him.

Whether it was the champagne or simply bowing to the inevitable, she found she no longer cared. 'You don't look so bad yourself,' she murmured, an involuntary sensual smile parting her soft lips. The formal silver-grey tailcoat and the intricately tied neckpiece gave him a slightly piratical air, and the familiar heightened awareness of him invaded her body. 'For an older man,' she dared to tease.

'I will remind you of that remark tonight,' Theo breathed huskily against her ear. 'Then we will see who has the most stamina,' he drawled, so seductively that desire ripped through her like a knife.

The music stopped, but Theo seemed reluctant to let her go. 'People are watching,' she said, lowering her eyes from his intense gaze, afraid he would see in her eyes the hunger and the need she was helpless to conceal.

She had watched him over the past week and she could not doubt his love for Stephen was absolute. As for her, she was just part of the package. To imagine otherwise would be fatal. Once before she had confused sex with Theo with love and she dared not make the same mistake again. But she had the uneasy feeling that it might already be too late... Was she already half in love with him? She didn't know, and she was glad of the diversion from her troubled thoughts when Tess appeared at her side and suggested it was time to change her outfit.

'No way.' Theo grinned easily down at Tess. 'No one is going to deprive me of the pleasure of unpeeling that spectacular dress from my wife's body. It has been driving me mad all day. I am whisking her off in the helicopter in ten minutes exactly as she stands.'

'A man after my own heart.' Tess laughed. 'If it wasn't for Bob, I would have had you myself.'

'Tess!' Willow remonstrated. What on earth got into her friend every time she saw Theo? She began flirting outrageously.

'Never mind the outrage, Willow. I have known you for years and you have hardly ever looked at another man, and now I know why. You were lucky; you started with the best. I knew the first time I clapped eyes on Theo he was Stephen's father and the only man for you. By the way, I have told your friend Dave that you were getting married so you have no need to worry on that score. Now off you go and enjoy your honeymoon. Stephen will be perfectly okay here with me and Bob and he has his pal Tommy to play with.'

Willow had forgotten all about Dave. Theo had swept every thought of the man out of her head. They had dated casually for over a year but she had never held any real feelings for him. More like just companionship.

'Forget Dave.' Theo swore softly. 'The helicopter is waiting.' Grasping her arm, and with a last hug and kiss for Stephen, he whisked her away. The congratulations of everyone was still ringing in her ears until they were drowned out by the sound of the rotary blades.

Situated on a spectacular headland, the hotel was out of this world. Their suite was magnificent but Willow was nervous. A glass wall opened out onto a fantastic terrace, and she wandered out to take a few deep steadying breaths of the warm night air, her eyes widening in awe at the fabulous view of the sea and the night sky.

'Champagne?' Theo suggested and came to stand behind her.

'This place is incredible, but where are we?' Willow asked. The flight had been barely half an hour, the helicopter had landed on the heli-pad and the manager of the hotel had met and escorted them straight to this lavish suite. She was alone with Theo for the first time in days, and fear and anticipation of the night ahead had made her as tense as a bowstring. 'Under the circumstances I don't think a honeymoon was really necessary,' she said stiffly.

His arm folded around her waist and he pulled her back against the hard lines of his powerful body. 'A very private hotel for the chosen few,' he said softly. 'Where it is does not matter—all you need to know is I have chosen you.' And turning her around in his arms, he added, 'As my wife.'

But he had not chosen her, Willow realised with an ache in her heart. Not really… He was as much a captive by the love he felt for his son as she was. Slowly she raised her head. Theo's lashes half covered his eyes, giving him a saturnine cast. Beneath them his gaze, intent and blatantly possessive, roamed over her face as his long fingers closed around her upper arms.

'And a honeymoon, although it will be unfortunately brief as I must be back in Athens on Monday, is a necessity to me,' Theo said, smiling his slightly crooked smile. 'Much as I love our son, we need some time alone together.' His dark eyes serious, he added, 'I want to make this marriage work. Surely you would not deny me the chance to try?'

Did he need her? Or would any woman do? she wondered. As for denying him! 'No,' she murmured. She wanted him too much. Then his hands slid gently up to cup her head in his palms and the depths of emotion in his night-black eyes, the intense raw passion, stunned her.

Willow stood very still, her breathing shaky. One week ago to this very day she had been an independent single mother, acclaimed by the press for her skill as a writer; now she was married to a man who offered her wealth and a basic primitive passion for a stipulated duration only. How had her world changed so dramatically? She instinctively tried to shake her head, her confusion showing in the blue eyes that clung to his.

Theo's dark head bent and he took her mouth in a kiss. It started as a gentle touch of his firm, silken lips against her own, and only ended when he had plunged deep and long into the moist depths, and Willow was boneless in his arms.

'Time to find the bedroom,' Theo suggested with a husky chuckle, swinging her up into his arms. Willow buried her face in his neck as he carried her into the bedroom. Slowly he lowered her down the long length of his body and she swayed as her feet touched the floor. Seconds later she gasped as he found the zip at the side of her wedding gown, and peeled it from her quivering body to fall in a pool of satin at her feet.

'I have ached to do that all day. The dress is exquisite, but you…' he husked throatily, and for a long moment he held her at arm's length. 'You are perfection.' His glittering black gaze swept down over her near-naked body, lingering on the firm, high breasts, her narrow waist, her only covering the briefest of silk lace briefs. When he lifted his head she saw the turbulence in the depths of his eyes, and her heart leapt.

He raised his hands to her hair and removed the clips holding it back almost reverently. He raked his fingers through the silken mass, and, lifting it to his face, he breathed deeply. 'I remember the scent of your hair from the first time we met, fresh apples in the fall. It is still the same,' he murmured huskily and, stepping back, smoothed the silken length over her shoulder.

He was right. 'Creature of habit, same shampoo,' she said softly, but she was touched by his memory. Maybe he did care for her a little, but he was not touching her now…and she needed him to, her senses inflamed by his unexpected mixture of tenderness and passion.

Then his dark head bent and he kissed her throat and scattered swift, biting kisses down the length of it as he divested himself of his clothes. Finally naked, he lifted his head, and he pressed a swift, hard kiss on her softly parted lips, his eyes dark as he reached for her shoulders.

'I thought I had imagined how smooth and white your skin was; a trick of memory, but I was wrong,' Theo murmured, his eyes roaming over her exposed flesh. 'Pale and translucent as a perfect pearl,' he husked, his hands gentle as he stroked slowly down over her firm breasts. The tips of his fingers began circling then teasing the burgeoning peaks before trailing down to shape her waist and lower to hook his thumbs in the scrap of lace and slip the last covering from her body.

Willow groaned her delight; she could not help it, her hands reaching to circle his neck. Did it really matter that she surrendered without a fight? Did it matter if it was only lust, or chemistry, even love…? He was her husband and, dear heaven, she wanted him. She tilted back her head for his kiss, her fingers threading through his hair and urging his head down, her lips softly parted in anticipation.

Theo obliged with the sweep of his tongue around the lush outline of her mouth, while his hand stroked and caressed a tantalising, subtle path down to the triangle of hair at the apex of her thighs. A long finger found the sensitive nub within, and he watched her incredible blue eyes widen and flare as he stroked with slow, sensual skill until he felt the tremors she could not control racing through her incredibly receptive body. His own heart pounding like a drum, he swung her up into his strong arms and laid her on the bed.

He was determined to make their wedding night unforgettable, and, after ravishing her mouth, he covered the pulse beating madly in her throat and sucked gently. Then he licked and kissed a slow, expert trail to her breast, delighting in the silken smoothness of her skin. He took one perfect rosy peak between his teeth and nipped gently, then began to suckle with greedy pleasure until he heard her feverish gasps of excitement. He relished the sound and transferred his attention to the other breast, with equally devastating results. His own skin began beading with sweat, his heart pounding as he moved lower to tease her navel and lower still to the juncture of her thighs.

She was hot, wet and wanting and went wild beneath

him. She wanted him inside her and he ached to be there, rock-hard and hurting. But he fought back the incredible urge, and, raising his head, he slipped his finger inside her. A triumphant primitive smile slashed his darkened features as he saw the pale beauty of her body suffused with colour, her blue eyes unfocussed and blind with passion.

At last she was his, her surrender complete. She was his wife. He kissed her hard with a dominant, possessive passion. 'Willow *mou,* all mine,' he groaned and, drawing back, he tilted her slender hips with hands that shook, and slowly thrust into her silken depths, and stilled.

'Theo…' Willow gasped, breathless as wave after wave of sensation buffeted her slender body. Delirious with excitement, she raked her hands down the solid wall of his chest and back again, her hand grasping his hip bones. 'Please,' she almost sobbed. It was like being tortured, held on the rack between pleasure and pain, but his hands tightened on her thighs, holding her still.

'Not yet,' Theo growled, his dark eyes intent on her, gauging her response to the nth degree. He slowly and skilfully took her to the edge and, testing his own control to the limit, he kept her there while he caught her whimpering cries with his mouth. With his tongue he did what her body, arching beneath him, was urging him to do with his own body. By a mighty effort of will he held back, and then once more tasted her luscious breasts before moving in her again. He felt her muscles clench around him and still he withdrew and waited, holding her on the pinnacle yet again.

'Please, please, Theo, don't stop,' Willow cried, her nails digging into his taut buttocks, her mouth urgently seeking his, her eyes closed. Breathless and out of her mind with excitement. 'Now…no…please, I can't…' she whimpered, incoherent in her need for his complete possession.

Hearing her pleading shattered Theo's control. He thrust

deep and hard, filling her to the hilt, his muscles locked, his great body taut as he thrust over and over again. Instantly she met and matched his rhythm and they rocketed over the edge, his seed shooting into her in a prolonged, explosive climax that left them both shuddering in the aftermath.

Later as the pounding of their hearts slowed Theo eased up and brushed the tumbled mass of hair back from her face and looked down at her. Her magnificent eyes, sated and slumberous, smiled lazily up at him.

'Wow,' she said dreamily.

'Wow—is that the best you can do as a writer?' he teased, and gently trailed a finger around her love-swollen lips.

'What do you expect when you have knocked every sensible thought from my brain?' Willow confessed, her breathing shallow but slowing.

'Good. I will have to make sure I keep you from thinking. That way our marriage will be fine.' And he fell back on the bed and slid an arm around her to cuddle her close to his side.

Even in her euphoric state she was taken aback by his statement and, rolling over to lean an arm on his chest, she looked lazily up at him. 'Do you really believe that a brainless wife makes for a good marriage? Is that why you divorced Dianne?' she asked without thinking. Immediately she felt the tension in him, and saw the hardening in his night-black eyes, and wished the words unsaid...

'Sorry. I should not have asked.' She withdrew her arm from his chest and turned onto her back. For a moment she had forgotten that theirs wasn't the kind of relationship that included sharing confidences.

'No, you shouldn't,' Theo said quietly, turning his head to glance across at her. 'But now you have perhaps it is as well you know the truth.' His dark eyes clashed with hers. 'I divorced Dianne because I caught her in bed with another man. So be warned.'

Whatever she had expected as a response, it was not that. She looked at him carefully. He was strikingly handsome, sinfully sexy and his great, tanned body simply oozed virile male power. He had to be joking, and Willow couldn't help but chuckle. 'I don't believe you. The other way around maybe.'

'Am I supposed to be flattered by that backhanded compliment?' Theo asked with a sardonic arch of one ebony brow.

'No, well, you know what I mean,' Willow muttered, suddenly realising he was not in the least amused.

'No, I don't know what you mean. Explain.' Theo leant up on one elbow, his dark eyes pinning her to the spot. 'Bearing in mind that adultery is not the sole prerogative of the male.'

'Yes, I know.' Suddenly she wished she had never started this conversation, but now she had... What the hell? She might as well tell the truth as she saw it. 'But let's be honest here, Theo, you're a very handsome man, very wealthy, and you must have had dozens of women over the years. Also given the fact that you were unfaithful with me when you were still engaged to Dianne and then married her anyway, the odds are that if anyone was going to stray in your marriage, you have to be the prime candidate.'

'Thank you for your opinion of me,' Theo ground out sarcastically. 'But you could not be more wrong. A, I was not engaged to Dianne when I slept with you, and B, I had finished with her the day before you and I met. Got it?'

Willow's eyes widened in stunned amazement. He looked so serious that she was inclined to believe him. Had she been wrong all those years ago?

'And, before you say anything, yes, I had spent the night before in Dianne's flat, but I had slept in the spare room. Because, and listen and learn, she tried to manipulate me using sex into giving her a commitment. I allow no woman to do that, not even you, my sweet wife.' The arrogant warning was evident in his dark eyes, and it surprised her.

'As if I could...' Willow said with a wry smile. Her knowledge of the male sex was so small she would not know where to start.

'You're a woman...' Theo drawled cynically. 'Anyway, I told Dianne it was over and I could not get away fast enough. Her frantic calls the next morning, one of which you apparently answered, were to try and get me back. I don't know what you said to her but you must have given her the idea that she had a rival.'

'I did nothing of the sort,' Willow exclaimed. 'I simply said you were still in bed asleep.'

'You said what?' Theo asked, his dark eyes widening incredulously, and then narrowing on her honest outraged blue. It was his turn to chuckle. *'Ah agape mou.'* He threaded long fingers through the silken waves of her hair, and lazily smoothed them over the curve of her breast. 'You really were an innocent. Surely you can see by telling her I was in bed asleep, you had as good as told her you had shared my bed.'

'Oh.' Willow stared back at Theo, feeling a fool. But with his hand on her breast it was a second or two before she could form any thoughts and get her vocal cords to work again. 'But you still married her,' she shot back. She wasn't that much of a fool...

'Yes, and do you know why?' Theo prompted, his eyes swirling for a moment with dark resentment. 'Because of you. Did it never cross your mind to wonder how I felt after you gave yourself to me, and then ran? I woke up the next morning to discover the woman I had asked to stay with me had gone. Then I had to discover from my sister you were only just eighteen and had in fact just left school that day.'

He was right—it had never once entered her head to think how he'd felt. 'I did wonder why you followed me to the airport,' she murmured.

'I followed you because I was mortified by what I had done, and I wanted to put it right. I wanted to see you again.' His long lashes lowered, masking his expression from her. 'I was twenty-eight and a bachelor at heart, but I had the mad idea that I might court you. But you soon put me right,' Theo drawled with dry self-mockery. 'Instead I spent the next three months drinking a bit too much and swinging between incredible anger that you could give away your innocence so lightly, and self-disgust that I had seduced someone so young.'

'I was eighteen, Theo, and you were right. It was only because I thought you were an unfaithful swine, a playboy who had women all over the place as well as a poor, long-suffering fiancée that I said what I did.'

'That is some impression I made on you,' he mocked, his eyes searching her expressive face, and he knew she was telling the truth. 'Not that it matters now.' He shrugged. 'But when you left, my ego took a serious knock. In fact you damn near unmanned me,' he said wryly. 'And let me assure you there was nothing long-suffering about Dianne—she was all over me like a rash. My ego duly restored, I married her.'

'That is terrible.' Willow stretched out an unsteady hand and placed it on his arm, her blue eyes full of sympathy gazing up into his. 'I had no idea.'

'Forget it,' Theo said bluntly. 'Your sympathy is misplaced. Dianne was a partner in the legal firm in New York that takes care of our business there, and the marriage was simply an extension of that partnership. It could have worked except, as I said, I returned home early from a trip abroad and caught her in bed with another man. We had been married for four years at the time, and with no sign of any children the divorce was no big deal,' he concluded dismissively.

At his reference to children Willow tensed, realising that she had discovered more about Theo in the last few minutes than he had ever told her before, but also that he had simply reaffirmed the real reason for their marriage: Stephen. She would be wise not to hope for too much, she reminded herself, but, looking up into his austerely handsome face, she felt the familiar twist of heat in her stomach that made her breath catch in her throat, and she could not tear her gaze away. She wanted his firm, sensuous mouth on her own again so badly, her mouth went dry, and her tongue flicked out to moisten her full bottom lip.

Theo studied her with brooding eyes. He saw the flick of her tongue, and the shimmer in her incredible blue eyes, and his darkening gaze dropped to the proud thrust of her exquisitely shaped breasts and the straining deep rose nipples. He wondered what the hell he was doing lying naked with his bride on his wedding night discussing a past disaster, when all he wanted to do was…

One hand looped around her neck, tangling in the tumbled mass of her hair, and he brought her head up, his mouth claiming hers with a driving hunger that made her moan in helpless pleasure. 'No more talking,' Theo rasped. 'I want you again now.'

Willow was more than happy to oblige, and helped him as he worked his erotic magic on every inch of her body. She eagerly returned the favour by teasing him, tasting him, shuddering on top of him, until a shattering climax caught her and all she could do was cry out and cling to him, lost in the realms of ecstasy she had never thought her body capable of.

In a hot, damp tangle of arms and legs she vaguely heard Theo mumble something in Greek, and then she was asleep.

'I've got to disguise this mark,' Willow said. 'A scarf, maybe.'

Theo was drinking a glass of champagne as she walked into the sitting room of their suite. He turned to face her, a look of amusement in his dark eyes, and studied her, his gaze narrowing on the hand she held to her neck.

'If you really want to go down to the dining room for lunch,' he commented, 'a scarf is not going to make much difference. All the staff are perfectly well aware we have not left the suite in three days. It does not take an Einstein to work out what we have been doing.'

Willow blushed scarlet and cursed her pale complexion. 'I know that, but we are leaving this afternoon and I haven't even seen the place yet. What will I say if Stephen or your mother asks me about the hotel?'

Theo laughed. 'My sweet, sexy wife, you worry too much.' Placing his glass down on the table, he reached for her and drew her into the circle of his arm. 'I own the place and I will fill you in on all the details on the way home tonight.' He took in the perfection of her pale features, the slight frown between her beautiful eyes. 'Now, where were we?' he murmured.

Willow gave him a luminous smile. 'You're insatiable.' She chuckled.

'And you love it,' Theo rasped, and dipped his head to capture the soft, sensual lips with his own.

Willow didn't see the rest of the hotel or the grounds, but as the manager escorted them to the heli-pad later that afternoon she glanced back at the long white building and knew she would remember it for the rest of her life.

It had been three days of sheer magic. She had seen a completely different side of Theo: the incredible lover, the amusing, attentive companion who had fed her every whim. They had taken their meals on the balcony and shared the huge spa bath. They had laughed, and talked about books, music and Stephen. And of course they had loved...

She glanced up at him, a faint reminiscent smile on her mouth as he said goodbye to the manager, her blue eyes wide and brilliant. Maybe their marriage was not the perfect storybook love match, but to her mind the past few days had come pretty close...

Sensing her gaze, Theo looked down at her, his smile quizzical. 'You look very pleased with yourself,' he said softly, and her beatific smile rocked him back on his heels. Yes. He had definitely made the right decision in marrying her. He had never had such incredible sex in his life. She was everything a woman should be.

It secretly thrilled him to watch her so coolly polite as she said her goodbye to the manager. She was a perfect lady, and only he knew she was an avid sensualist in bed, the perfect mate, in fact. As if that weren't enough for any man, the icing on the cake was Stephanos.

Slipping an arm around her slender shoulders, he led her to the waiting helicopter. Willow had given him a wonderful son, and he hoped for one or two more. The future looked rosy, except for one unpleasant duty he had yet to perform...

CHAPTER ELEVEN

'DO YOU really have to go to work so early?' Willow asked, watching Theo as he donned the garb of a successful tycoon.

'Yes, I do.' Theo slipped on the jacket of the slate-grey suit and glanced across at Willow lying on the bed. The sheet that was draped across her slender hips did not reach her navel. He let his eyes roam over the smooth sweep of her elegant body, enjoying the sexy picture she presented. 'Tempting as you are, lover, the unexpected break in my schedule has left me with a lot of work to catch up on, but later in the year I promise we will have a proper honeymoon.'

'There was nothing improper about our honeymoon.' She smiled slowly, remembering. 'It was great.'

One dark brow arched with sardonic amusement 'If that was you behaving properly, I can hardly wait to discover what the improper Willow is capable of.' And he chuckled at her sudden blush. 'But wait I must because unfortunately I have a business dinner to attend this evening, so I am afraid you will have to dine without me.'

Abruptly Willow sat up. 'What time will you be back?'

'I don't know, but not too late,' Theo said, avoiding her gaze. 'But tomorrow we are moving to my home and this will be the last day you and Stephanos will have with my mother for a while. She is going to America to visit old friends for a month or two, so enjoy it while you can. The few things you have here can be packed in the morning and all the rest of your things from England I had transported over with Tess last week, and it is already at my home.'

'We are not living here?' Willow said, shocked by the turn of events.

Theo slanted her a look of mocking amusement. 'Come on, Willow, you must have realised we are not staying here. I have not lived with my mother in almost twenty years.'

Disconcerted, Willow murmured, 'I never thought...' She wasn't sure she liked the idea that he had had her home in England stripped of her possessions.

'I've told you before, don't think and we will get along fine,' he declared arrogantly, and with a brief kiss on the top of her head he left.

With Judy's reassurance that she would love her new home and that it was only a few short miles from hers, Willow had forgotten all about Theo's rather abrupt departure that morning. They took their seat for the start of the *Son et Lumière* over the Acropolis. It had been Judy's suggestion to see the show, and then eat out, and Willow had jumped at the chance.

Later, as they were sitting around the dining table in an exclusive restaurant, overlooking the Parthenon, Willow laughed as Stephen wrinkled his nose at the octopus Judy was urging him to taste. Later still, having devoured a delicious dessert of sweet pastry, ice cream and exotic fruit, Willow sighed her contentment as she sipped her coffee. 'That was a marvellous meal. I could not eat another thing.'

Judy grinned. 'You're lucky you're not the type to put on weight, but me...' She pulled a face and laughed.

'Look.' Stephen leapt to his feet. 'It's Daddy!' He ran across the restaurant towards the entrance.

Willow was sitting with her back to the room, and just before she rose to her feet to catch Stephen she saw Judy's head jerk up. She thought she saw a flicker of either fear or fury in the older woman's eyes but she wasn't sure which. She must have been mistaken because a second later Judy was again smiling at her.

'Why, yes, it is, what a nice surprise.'

Willow turned around, and walking towards her was Theo. On one side of him was Stephen and on the other side, with her hand on his arm, was a very striking woman. She was small with short blonde spiky hair and was dressed in a skimpy pink metal-studded designer suit. Some business meeting, Willow thought scathingly, and out of nowhere jealousy as sharp as a knife almost sliced her in two. Oh, no… She almost groaned out loud. She couldn't, she mustn't be falling in love with her arrogant husband. But why else would she be racked by jealousy at the sight of him with another woman? She looked up at Theo through the thick veil of her lashes attempting to hide the hurt in her eyes, but she could tell nothing from his expression.

'This is a pleasant surprise, darling,' Theo offered, lowering his head to press a swift kiss to her smooth cheek before he turned to smile at Judy. 'Mother…I had no idea you were planning a night on the town. You know Christine, don't you?' Judy smiled at the other woman and addressed her in Greek.

Willow stood feeling like an Amazon next to the small blonde. Dressed as she was, in a denim skirt and simple white scoop-necked top, she also felt at a distinct disadvantage. Theo's cutting comment about her dress sense rose up to haunt her. When she finally looked around the circle of faces she was aware of a subtle tension in the air and then Theo affected an introduction.

'Willow this is Christine Markham. She runs a very successful interior design business, ''Chrismark International Interiors''. You might have heard of them.'

Willow held out her hand and made the polite response. 'Nice to meet you.'

'My pleasure.' Christine's hand barely touched hers as she gushed, 'Theo has told me so much about you. I've been dying to meet you.' She took in Willow's simple clothes and unruly hair with a look of sheer derision in her dark eyes.

At that information Willow stiffened, and slanted a glance up at her indomitable husband. How dared he discuss her with another woman? She saw a faint flush on his cheekbones before his features hardened into an inscrutable mask. Underneath the calm exterior of her face her mind was working feverishly. Was Theo ashamed of her or was he cheating on her or both? And she nearly brought back the meal she had just eaten, the acrid taste of jealousy making her feel sick.

God! If this was what love did to someone, Willow realised she did not want to know...it was far too painful. So she did what she always did and resorted to icy politeness.

'Has he? How nice,' she said in her cool, well-mannered voice. 'Unfortunately he has never mentioned you to me, so I cannot return the favour.' It was catty, she knew, but she did not care.

'Christine has just returned from New York where her firm has completed the revamping of one of our hotels, Willow, darling,' Theo said smoothly, his eyes narrowing on her pale face. 'Successfully, I hope. This is a business dinner to fill me in on the final details.'

It wasn't exactly a lie, but neither was it the whole truth, and Theo cursed the bad luck that had allowed them to bump into each other like this. But how did one admit to one's wife—I am sorry, my mistress was away when we were married and I had to meet her, tell her it is all over and pay her off.

'Yes, so you told me this morning,' she said coolly, slightly mollified but not totally convinced. She glanced back at Judy, looking for reassurance, and was relieved to see even his mother was smiling, completely unconcerned, so it must be okay.

It was her totally unexpected stupid jealousy that was making her read things into the situation that were not there, she told herself. And none of her troubled thoughts showed in her face as she looked up at Theo again.

'In that case, don't let us stop you,' she said firmly. 'We have finished our meal and I only have to pay the bill. Anyway it is time I got Stephen home to bed.'

Theo was torn between anger and embarrassment, and his mother's reproachful eyes didn't help, nor did the innocent acceptance in his wife's and son's. But not by a flicker of an eyelash did he show his discomfort.

Instead, his dark eyes softening on Willow's beautiful face, he smiled down into her trusting sapphire eyes and said, 'I'll take care of the bill, and you take care of Stephanos and Mother. Watch her driving—she can be lethal when the mood strikes her.' Reaching to tuck a tendril of hair behind her ear in a tender gesture, he added huskily, 'I'll see you later; wait for me.'

Willow did…and he made love to her with a gentle passion like nothing that had gone before, and all her doubts were laid to rest.

Six weeks later Willow sat in front of the dressing-table mirror and applied the final coat of lip gloss to her full lips. Theo had called her from his office in Athens to tell her he would be home soon. Tonight they were going to a reception at the British Embassy for some visiting international businessmen. Charles had also called her earlier and reminded her to bring him another one of her books for his mother. They had become quite friendly over the weeks, and Theo didn't mind because he knew Charles was gay.

Slipping the lipstick into the small drawer under the mirror, her fingers lingered on the tape of her birth-control pills. Withdrawing them, she hesitated, a musing smile on her face as she turned the strip over in her hand. Maybe now was the time to throw them away. Theo need never know she had ever taken them.

Her marriage was going much better than she could have ever hoped. The past few weeks had been almost perfect. Stephen had settled into Greek life incredibly well. It must have something to do with his genes but he was picking up the Greek language with an amazing ease. He adored his father, as did Willow, she freely admitted, her blue eyes dreamy.

Theo was a wonderful lover and an attentive husband. He had made no complaint when she had asked if they could make a quick trip back to England to see her publisher, but had turned it into a four-day holiday for all three of them. He showered her in presents, from the diamond hair-clips for her wedding present to a diamond pendant that matched her engagement ring to mark the one-week anniversary of their marriage, a fully fitted study to enable her to continue with her writing to the single rose bought from a street seller when they dined out—he spoilt her rotten.

She had tried to remonstrate with him when he had opened a bank account in her name with an enormous amount of money, and insisted on giving her a monthly allowance. It was the nearest they had come to an argument, and of course he had won by the simple expedient of making love to her. And in that department, incredibly, it just kept getting better and better, the intimacy and the caring between them growing by the day.

Mia, his housekeeper, was a brilliant cook and, with the help of her husband and two daily maids, the house ran like clockwork. Tonight Stephen was staying with his grandmother and Mia and her husband were having the night off so the house seemed eerily quiet.

As she glanced around the room Willow's smile faded somewhat. The only fly in the ointment was this house. She had recognised it as soon as she'd walked in the door. It was the house Theo had built for Dianne, and however much she tried to tell herself that it did not matter, it did. The house itself was magnificent and the grounds extensive. The security was second only to Fort Knox, but deep down inside it bothered her. She didn't like the feeling of being caged in a house that had been built for another woman.

She hadn't mentioned it to Theo, even though with every passing day she was becoming more and more confident in their marriage. She thought the closeness growing between them was too new for her to risk spoiling it.

She grimaced. Perhaps next month… She took a pill and headed for the bathroom and a glass of water.

'I hope the water running means what I think it means.' Theo's deep, melodious voice had her spinning round and she almost dropped the glass she was holding. A tide of red washed over her pale features. He had shed his business suit, shirt and tie and, with his thumbs in the waistband of his black boxers, he looked incredibly attractive, his dark eyes roaming over her tall, elegant body with obvious sensual intent.

'I didn't hear you arrive. I was just getting a glass of water—I was thirsty,' she said hurriedly.

He gave her a quizzical glance, taking in her lightly made-up face, the mass of black hair pinned on top of her head, the diamond pendant he had bought her nestling in the slight shadow of her breasts. She was wearing a shimmering silver evening dress that slashed across under her arms, and revealed every curve of her delectable body, ending a couple of inches above her knees and exposing the long length of her legs. It crossed his mind that if he had had any sense at all he would have kept her in her long, all-encompassing cotton dresses. She was far too delectable to be exposed to other men's eyes.

A wry smile quirked his mouth and he sighed. 'Ah, I am too late. You look absolutely divine. The skirt's a bit short maybe... And I was hoping to join you in the shower.' Moving towards her, he dropped a kiss on her brow. 'Out, before I change my mind.' He tapped her on the bottom, and stripped off his shorts.

For a moment Willow simply stared. The light caress of his mouth across her brow and his magnificent tanned, naked body, already hardening in arousal, had her melting inside as always.

'Or perhaps you would care to change it for me?' Theo said with a husky laugh.

'What?' She lifted her mesmerised eyes to his and saw his pupils darken and dilate. She had to forcibly remind herself that they were supposed to be on their way out. 'No, you devil,' she said with a shake of her head and a reluctant grin, and headed for the door.

'I'll get you later and that is a promise.' Theo's laughing shout followed her into the bedroom.

'I will meet you downstairs,' she teased back. 'I don't trust you in a bedroom.' Later she would realise how cruelly true her parting shot had been...

It was a glittering affair and, because Willow's childhood years had included holidaying with her mother at various embassies around the world, she felt quite comfortable in such a gathering. The Foreign Office was quite a close-knit community and she had been both surprised and delighted when she had met the British Ambassador to Greece at a dinner some weeks ago, only to discover that he had known her mother and her father.

The cream of Greek society mingled with British and other Europeans, plus a smattering of Americans. There was no trouble with the language as virtually everyone spoke English. Everyone except for a huge businessman from Russia, who devoured Willow with his eyes when they were introduced. She had no trouble knowing exactly what he was thinking, but Theo led her away with a whispered comment in her ear that the man was rumoured to be the head of the Russian Mafia.

A host of willing waiters circulated champagne and canapés, and Willow was really enjoying herself. Leo was there and was at his outrageous best, chatting up every good-looking woman in sight.

Christine Markham caused a sensation in a white satin slip of a dress, that plunged at the back and front, and was transparent enough to show the dark centres of her breasts.

With Theo's arm around her, Willow glanced up at him, her blue eyes lit with amusement. 'You thought my dress was too short. Do you think Christine knows hers is almost see-through?'

'Oh, she knows, all right,' Theo murmured with a sardonic arch of one eyebrow. 'Believe me.' And he thanked his lucky stars that he had not made the serious mistake of proposing to the woman. She was a dyed-haired, dyed-in-the-wool career woman. A good decorator, but as hard as steel.

'There you are, Willow.' Charles appeared, his boyish face creased in a smile. 'Have you remembered the book you promised me for my mother?'

'Yes, of course.' She smiled back. 'I—'

'Charles,' Theo cut in. 'Look after my wife for me a moment. I've just seen Stavros arrive and I want to have a private word with him.' Glancing down at Willow, his dark eyes apologetic, he said, 'Do you mind, Willow? A little business I need to attend to.'

'Of course not. According to the invitation that is what the evening is for.' She smiled mischievously up at him. 'I can read, and I can look after myself for five minutes, you know.'

Her comment brought a glint of humour to his eyes and something more. 'I know,' Theo said, lifting his long fingers and curving the line of her jaw, something reflective visible in his intent gaze. 'I don't know what I did to deserve you, but I thank God every day,' and, dropping the lightest of kisses on her soft lips, he let her go. 'I won't be long, darling.' And he moved swiftly away through the crowd.

'Yuk, married love—very touching,' Charles drawled mockingly. 'But what about the book, Willow? I am going back to England on Saturday.'

'I left it in the ladies' cloakroom with my shawl. Wait here and I'll get it for you.'

'I'll come with you. I wouldn't dare defy an order from Theo. Such a shame he is so rampantly heterosexual, I've always thought.'

'Charles, you're incorrigible.' Willow was still grinning as she entered the cloakroom, leaving Charles leaning against the wall outside.

The cloak deposit desk was separated from the rest of the room by a seven-foot-high latticed partition that formed an L shape and hid the washbasins from view. She gave the attendant her ticket and waited while the woman disappeared into what looked like a dark hole. Willow idly glanced up at the magnificent plaster ceiling high above.

The embassy had been built in a different era. It was a huge gracious Georgian building, and it was good to see it had been adapted sensitively to modern needs.

Then she heard Theo's name mentioned and her ears instinctively pricked up.

'Theo Kadros has behaved absolutely appallingly, Christine. He is a complete bastard; after all, it was common knowledge you and he were going to marry. I don't know how you can be so brave.'

What little colour Willow had instantly drained from her face. She knew the voice she could hear was Charles's secretary. Willow had spoken to her a couple of times on the telephone, and had met her at the same dinner at which she'd met the Ambassador. She was a thirty-something Englishwoman and according to Charles was noted for being a terrible gossip.

'I don't have much choice.' Christine's accented English was unmistakable. 'I can compete with any woman, but with an eight-year-old son I stood no chance.'

'It must have been a terrible shock for you returning to Athens and discovering he had married again.'

'Not really. Theo rang me while I was in New York, and said he had something to tell me and we arranged a date to meet. Then of course everyone was talking about his engagement party. By the time I actually met Theo for dinner it was the day after he got back from his honeymoon; I pretty much knew what to expect. But Theo, ever the gentleman, explained everything to me. I even met his new wife and son at the restaurant.'

'Ah, like that, is it?' The salacious eagerness in the voice made Willow's stomach turn. 'I might have guessed. Dianne divorced him not long after you decorated her house, as I recall. History repeating itself, perhaps.'

The attendant returned with the book and numbly Willow

took it from her, not saying a word as she listened to Christine's reply.

'Let's just say he gave me this diamond necklace after dinner, and things are not over yet,' Christine said archly and laughed.

Willow did not need to hear any more. Silently she ran from the cloakroom and straight past Charles. She saw an open French door, and darted through into the garden. Taking in great gulping breaths of the night air, Willow tried to fight down the nausea that threatened to overwhelm her. She began to shake and she could not stop.

Images of her honeymoon, of lying in the huge bed with Theo, with their bodies entwined. Herself, a willing and wanton partner in all his erotic love-making. These images now turned her stomach as they were overlaid by others of Theo doing exactly the same thing to Christine only the very next day after they returned.

How could he? her heart cried. What kind of sadistic monster was he that he'd even had the nerve to introduce her to the woman when they had met in the restaurant? She saw again the fleeting look in his mother's eyes, which she had dismissed at the time, and she groaned out loud. Even his own mother knew and had said nothing. And worse still…later Theo had had the gall to come straight from his mistress's bed to hers. She had stupidly believed that his unexpected gentle passion had been because he truly cared for her, when in reality it had probably been because he'd been exhausted!

Willow could not believe how stupid she had been. What kind of prize idiot was she? She had actually thought she was falling in love with Theo all over again and had fooled herself into thinking that he might feel the same. The tears rolled down her cheeks unchecked as she faced the agonising truth. She did love him, probably always had and always would. A man less worthy of love would be impossible to find and she felt her heart break and shatter into a million pieces. She pushed her clenched fist into her mouth and bit down hard on her knuckle to prevent herself from screaming her anguish out loud.

CHAPTER TWELVE

'WILLOW, what is wrong?' Charles's lanky figure appeared at her side. 'What's the matter? You're shivering.' His long arm swept around her shoulders, hugging her to him.

She looked up at him, her eyes swimming in tears. 'Please, Charles, get me out of here,' she whispered, her voice breaking on a sob.

'You are upset; I'd better go and get Theo.'

'No, no, not him, never him,' she cried.

'Okay, okay, if you say so. I'll take you to my office and then you can tell me what happened.' Leading her around the building and through another door, he finally settled her onto a sofa in his office. 'You look like you could use a brandy.' Crossing to his desk, he withdrew a bottle from the drawer and filled a small tumbler. 'I keep this here for medicinal purposes only, you understand,' he said, flashing her a smile.

She looked up into his friendly face and, taking the glass he held out for her, she downed its contents in one go. The fiery liquid burnt her throat, but it had the desired effect and slowly her shivering ceased.

'Are you sure you don't want me to get Theo? Did someone attack you?'

'No,' she said, roughly wiping the tears from her eyes with the back of her hand.

'Then what is it, Willow? What happened?' Charles sat down beside her and placed a comforting arm around her shoulders. With his other hand he removed the book she was still clenching in her fingers. 'You've got my book.

Surely you can't be that upset at having to give one away,' he tried to tease.

White-faced she looked at him with dull blue eyes, all the brilliance gone. 'No.' She tried to smile, but her lips trembled and she had to blink back more tears. 'Something much worse.' She had fallen in love and given away her heart and her life to a man without a shred of morality; a man who had used her quite ruthlessly for his own convenience.

With that knowledge came the dawning realisation over and above her own shock and despair that the time was past for her to procrastinate as she usually did. For the sake of her own pride and self-esteem she had to face the problem head-on; she refused to be any man's fool—she was worth more than that.

'Charles, you're a friend, and you have lived in Athens for years,' she said slowly, battling the tremor in her voice. She needed to know the truth. No more hoping for love…fooling herself…it was over…and her broken heart congealed into a hard lump of stone in her breast.

'Five, to be precise,' Charles answered.

'Then will you do something for me?'

'Anything for you.' He grinned.

'Tell me the truth?' Willow asked, her eyes as hard and cold as the blue diamond she wore on her finger. 'About Christine and Theo.' She did not really need to go on. Charles was cursed with the same complexion as her and a dull stain of red covered his pale face. 'How long has it been going on? Is it true Theo was planning to marry her, until I appeared with Stephen?'

'So that's it. I saw Christine come out of the cloakroom straight after you.'

'Please, Charles, I want to know it all from the very beginning.' She rested a hand on his arm. 'Did Theo di-

vorce his first wife for adultery?' She saw the genuine surprise in his eyes. 'I thought not.' So that was another of
Theo's lies. How many more had he told? she wondered
bitterly. Then the shock that had frozen her emotions gave
way to ice-cold fury. The arrogant, lecherous swine of a
man, the no-good, double-dealing bastard! 'Come on,
Charles, I want to know everything.'

His pale eyes looked compassionately into hers. 'It is
only gossip, Willow—rumour, if you like. Apparently
Dianne had hired Chrismark International Interiors to re-
decorate the house in Greece a year or so after she married
Theo. Dianne was a woman who liked constant change,
some said also in the bedroom, but I don't know about that.
All I do know is Dianne and Theo became friends with
Christine and of course they socialised together. Some say
Dianne caught Theo with Christine in their bed, a few say
it was the other way around and he caught Dianne with
another man, take your pick. But, in all fairness, it was a
no-fault divorce. It could all be lies, but Dianne went back
to America.

'Theo had a couple of relationships with other women
and then a year or so ago he began escorting Christine
around. There was probably nothing in the rumours about
them at the time of the divorce. Anyway, it was all very
civilised, and in her professional capacity Dianne still does
business with Theo's companies. When he is in New York
some say she does more than that, but it is all just gossip.'

'You still have not answered my first question. Was Theo
going to marry Christine?'

'What can I say?' He grimaced. 'Except, Christine certainly thought so, by all accounts.'

'Especially your secretary's.'

'Yes, but, Willow, Theo married you. I am sure you're
making a fuss over nothing. I am not into women, but no

man would want the Christines of this world if they could have a beautiful, talented, intelligent girl like you, and Theo Kadros is no fool.'

'No, he isn't. But I am,' she said bitterly. Charles had simply confirmed what she had guessed was true.

'Don't even think like that Willow. You are nobody's fool,' Charles said, rising to his feet. 'And what is more you are going to prove it. There is a washroom through there. He indicated a door. 'Spruce yourself up and let's get back. You are British, stiff bottom lip and all that, remember...'

Willow stared at her reflection in the bathroom mirror, her blue eyes dulled with pain. She had known from the very beginning that she was not cut out for Theo's sophisticated, amoral lifestyle. Their relationship had been a disaster in the making from the very start, and it was time she cut her losses and left.

Dear heaven, if the gossip was true, her fiend of a husband had slept with Christine and his ex-wife... Quickly she repaired her make-up, new steel now entering her spine. The pain would return, she knew, but first she was going to ditch her disreputable husband once and for all.

Ten minutes later she walked back into the main reception room, arm in arm with Charles. The first person Willow spotted was Theo standing in a group that included the ambassador and his wife. The couple standing next to him, Charles told her, was a man called Stavros, then his wife Alethea, and next to them stood Christine.

The sight of Theo in Christine's company served to stiffen her spine still further and feed her anger. My God! They were so blatant; had they no shame? A man like Theo obviously considered himself above the emotions of mere mortals. He took what he wanted without thought or consequence.

'Has Theo read all of your books?' Charles asked softly.

'What?' She glanced up in surprise. 'No, I don't think so.'

'Perfect. Attack is the best form of defence, so why not go for it?' Charles grinned down at her.

'I don't know what you mean,' Willow murmured.

'How do you feel about making a fool out of your arrogant husband for a change?' Charles said, his pale eyes dancing mischievously down at her. 'I have read all three of your books, and in the first one the villain is quite obviously taken from real life.' He nodded towards Theo. 'And I bet he has no idea.'

Charles was right; she had used Theo as her villain in her first book, and she was pretty sure he didn't know. Theo had only read her last book. Surprising he'd had time to do that given the numerous women he kept, she thought venomously.

'Good, follow my lead,' Charles commanded, and it was pride alone that carried her forward.

'Willow, darling.' Theo's head turned as they approached. 'I wondered where you and Charles had got to.' She was almost fooled all over again by the warmth in his smile...but not quite.

'My fault, Theo. I persuaded Willow to tell me about her work and it was so enthralling we lost track of time,' Charles replied.

'You're highly honoured,' Theo said smoothly, his dark enquiring eyes on Willow. 'Usually she refuses to discuss her work.' Willow knew what he meant—she had told him once after making love that she never discussed her storylines until she was finished. He had laughed and said she was a secretive little thing and they had made love again.

'Charles can be very insistent,' she said coolly, ignoring Theo and smiling at Charles.

'I shall have to discover his secret.' Theo chuckled, and added, 'Alethea has been longing to meet you; apparently she is a big fan of yours, and has read all of your books.' He slipped an arm around her waist, a confident smile on his firm lips.

Willow's slender body tensed at his casual embrace and she concentrated her attention on Alethea as the introduction was made. She couldn't bear to look into her husband's lying eyes.

'Then you must have recognised Alethea,' Charles cut in with a charming smile for the older woman, 'that villain in the first book was obviously taken from someone we all know.' He laughed and gave a telling glance at Theo.

'But of course,' Alethea exclaimed and grinned at Theo. 'I'm amazed you let her get away with it, Theo.' She chuckled out loud.

Theo's dark eyes narrowed cautiously. 'With what?'

'Don't tell me you have not read all of Willow's books?' Charles mocked lightly.

'Guilty as charged. I have only read her latest. As a newly married man I have been much too busy to read,' he said smoothly, and tightened his arm around Willow's waist, slanting a gleaming smile at her, but she avoided his eyes.

'Then you don't know that the description of the serial killer is you to a T,' Charles teased.

She sensed rather than saw Theo's head jerk up. She had never expected anyone to make the connection before but now she was glad they had.

'Is that right, Willow, darling?' Theo was taken aback. A murderer? Surely she had not hated him that much. He was oddly hurt, but he was damned if he was going to show it. 'I am so glad to be of help,' he commented as with his free hand he tilted her chin so she had to look at him.

'I admit it,' she said offhandedly, and the eyes that met his were cool. 'But then we writers have to get our inspiration from somewhere.' She smiled.

All Theo's male antennae rose in red alert as he noted the faint shadows beneath her eyes, and the slightly too bright smile. Something was badly wrong with his lovely wife, and he let his hand fall from her face. In the next few minutes he found out exactly what.

'You'd better beware, Theo,' Charles jocularly remarked in his cut-glass English accent. 'Her next one is about a woman who murders her husband.'

'How exciting. Can you tell us more, Willow?' Alethea asked, her brown eyes keen with interest.

'Oh, I don't know.' Willow let her glance skim around the group, her eyes glancing off the necklace around Christine's throat, and it gave her an idea.

'Well, maybe a little,' she said, and with vengeance in mind she did what she did best...let her imagination run riot...

'It starts with the woman finding a receipt in her husband's pocket for a diamond necklace.' And she let her gaze linger for a moment on Christine. 'Something glamorous like yours, Christine.' She smiled coolly, and was gratified to see the shock in Christine's face.

She didn't look at Theo but she almost laughed out loud at the sudden tension she could sense in every line of his long body. Yes, you bastard, squirm, she thought bitterly and continued, beginning to enjoy herself.

'But the wife knew that her husband had certainly not bought it for her, so she realises that he must have a mistress. Then she discovers he has not one, but two, and he had the colossal arrogance to marry her while keeping both of them. As you would expect, the wife's upset turns to murderous rage, and she determines to dispose of him, but craftily and at no threat to herself...'

It had gone very silent. Everyone in the group was waiting for what would happen next, and at least two of them more in fear than interest.

'I think that is enough.' Theo's fingers dug threateningly into her waist. 'You don't want to give away the whole plot, Willow, darling.'

'Spoilsport, Theo,' Charles spoke up. 'It sounds absolutely intriguing. I'm sure we all want to discover how it ends.' His golden eyes gleamed with amused respect at Willow. 'Do continue.'

'Oh, but she must get caught in the end,' Alethea said, totally unaware of the undercurrents swirling beneath the conversation as she addressed Willow again. 'If I remember rightly, in the first one the serial killer got the electric chair, and in the next a life sentence. Your murderers always do.'

'Maybe, maybe not,' Willow responded enigmatically. Only then did she tilt her chin to look up at Theo. A muscle was pulsing in his jaw, his mouth a grim line, and there was a ruthlessness in the dark eyes. But she didn't care; his reaction was proof, if any more proof were needed, she thought scathingly. 'But you are right, darling, I must not give any more away.' And she didn't just mean the plot.

'Very wise,' Theo responded with a sardonic tilt of one dark brow. But he was furiously angry that she had dared to assault his character in front of Greek society's élite. She knew exactly what she was doing even though most of what she was saying was fiction.

How she had found out about the necklace he did not know; she had certainly never discovered any receipt. But one glance at her face as she'd looked at Christine, her cool blue gaze lingering on the necklace, it was blatantly obvious that she knew. Willow was a strong, proud woman, and she had struck back at him in her own unique way, he had to give her that. But right now he felt more like throttling her, and his main priority was to get her out of here.

The chauffeur manipulated the limousine through the Athens traffic, and Willow sat in the back seat determinedly looking out of the window in stony silence. Theo had not said a word since they had left the reception together. But she could feel the tension, the simmering anger, pulsing in the air between them, and she knew the only thing preventing him from reacting was the presence of the driver.

The car eventually slowed and the driver activated the security gates. Within minutes they reached the entrance to the villa, and the car stopped.

Theo leapt out before the driver could even move and was already opening the door beside Willow. 'Out,' he said and grabbed her arm, and told the driver to leave.

He urged her up the steps to the massive front doors of the villa, and quickly opened them, bundling her inside, and only then did he set her free.

Theo turned as Willow was walking away from him and he opened his mouth to yell at her, but then stopped. By a supreme effort of will he managed to control his temper. She had tried to make a fool of him in front of their friends and no one got away with that. But as his gaze slid over her proud dark head he saw the tension in the slender shoulders. He realised with a sickening jolt in his chest that what he had done to her was as bad, if not worse. He had used her love for her child to force her into marriage, and, in his conceit, had presumed that as long as he showered her in presents and kept her satisfied in bed, she would be a happy and dutiful wife.

He was so used to sophisticated women in his life, and always had been. In his world when an affair started and ended a suitable pay-off was expected and usually given.

People changed partners regularly but, with cynical disregard of any finer feelings, continued to mix socially with no apparent hard feelings on either side. In his arrogance he had made no allowance for the fact that Willow was not one of them. The women he had known in the past would not have cared if they had met one of his exes wearing diamonds he had given them, as long as they were the one in favour at the time, and that eventually they too would get their share.

His dark brows drew together in a frown. Willow was not like that; she took more pleasure from a single rose than she did from a fortune in diamonds. And if he ever found out who had told her about Christine's necklace he would destroy them. But in the meantime, unless he was very careful, Willow would walk away from him for good and that was something he could not contemplate. She was young, beautiful and talented and earned a good living. She didn't need him half as much as he needed her and the knowledge hit him like a thunderbolt. He loved her...

Willow made her away across the massive reception hall heading for the stairs. She had nothing to say to Theo. She entered the master suite, and, grabbing her nightgown off the bed, she just as quickly exited. She made her way to the guest room as far away as possible from the room she had shared with Theo. There were plenty to choose from, she thought bitterly. The house was like a mausoleum, and tonight had certainly seen the death of all her hopes.

She pushed open a door into an elegant blue and white bedroom and noted the queen-sized bed. It was more than big enough for her, and she crossed into the stark white *ensuite* bathroom. She quickly shrugged off her dress and briefs and slipped the nightgown over her head. Then she swiftly removed her make-up, unpinned her hair and shook it free.

It crossed her mind why Theo had not followed her, and then she berated herself for being so weak. Why should he? He knew she had found him out. He no longer had to pretend he cared...

She walked back into the bedroom and froze. Theo was standing in the middle of the room wearing only a black silk robe, tall and infinitely formidable, his chiselled features set in a hard, impenetrable mask.

Theo's control had been stretched to the limit after he had walked into their bedroom, determined to be reasonable, and found her gone. He had told himself to calm down, stripped and quickly showered. Willow wasn't going anywhere tonight—the house was locked up as tight as a drum. He would find her and explain that Christine meant nothing to him, less than nothing, and make her understand. But looking at her cool, pale face and her luscious body covered in a swirl of violet silk that floated to her feet, her blue eyes openly defying him, he wanted to shake her until her teeth rattled.

'What do you think you are doing, Willow?' he demanded in a dangerously quiet voice. 'You are my wife, and you sleep in my bed.'

'Not any more,' Willow said bluntly. 'The marriage is over.' Her mind was made up. She should never have married the heartless swine in the first place. Millions of children lived with divorced parents, and, while she would never have wished it on her son, she was not the type to be a martyr.

Theo's expression changed to one of sardonic cynicism. 'I think not, but obviously we need to talk. That overactive imagination of yours appears to have developed some very strange ideas.'

'There was nothing strange about the diamond necklace around your mistress's throat; in fact it was quite beautiful.'

She matched him for cynicism. 'And the only strange idea is yours, that you should imagine for a second that I would ever share a bed with you again.' Willow drew in a deep unsteady breath, and managed to keep her voice cool with the greatest difficulty. 'Now, please leave.'

In two lithe strides he reached her and caught her shoulders in a bruising grip. 'Let go of me, Theo.'

'Never,' he rasped. 'I have only one question for you, Willow. Who told you about Christine? And, so help me, I will destroy them. Can't you see that they were only trying to make trouble between us, you little fool?'

Calling her a fool was like waving a red rag to a bull. Willow retaliated without thought of the consequences. 'I might be a fool but it was you that made me one!' And her usual cool voice shook with rage. 'My God, you bullied me into marrying you, and then had the colossal nerve to introduce me to your mistress. Not just me, but my son, and all the while your own mother was looking on, and even she knew. Well, let me tell you something.' She poked a finger in his chest. 'You have made a fool of me for the last time, Theo. I am out of here tomorrow, and you can go to hell.'

'If I do then you are damn well coming with me.' Theo's black eyes gleamed with frustrated fury and she gave a silent cry of pain as his hands tightened on her slender shoulders.

'For God's sake, Willow, grow up and enter the real world. So what if Christine was my mistress? I'm a thirty-seven-year-old man. What the hell did you expect? You and I met again by accident—I did not have a chance to finish with Christine before we got married. What you saw at the restaurant *was* business in a way. I was telling her at the first opportunity I had that it was over and paying her off, and she knew it. I had not slept with her in over two months.'

'And that makes it all right, then?' she prompted mockingly. 'My God, you are despicable.' Her blue eyes blazed with bitter contempt.

'Despicable maybe, but at least I had the decency to tell Christine to her face it was over. You on the other hand allowed your friend to inform your lover Dave for you,' he taunted. 'How despicable is that?'

'Dave was never my lover!' She was so outraged that he had dared to try and make this her fault that she told him much more than she had intended.

'I have never had a lover. I never had the time, I was too busy looking after my son and earning a living.' She gave a choked laugh. 'Much good it did me. You barged back into my life, stole my son, and stuck me in this—' she glanced wildly around the luxuriously appointed room '—great mausoleum of a house, that you had built for your first wife and decorated by your mistress.'

His hands tightened into an excruciating grip. 'I never—'

'Don't bother denying it, Theo.' She cut him off and met his narrowed gaze, her own eyes blazing. 'I saw the article in the magazine all those years ago, featuring this house and Dianne. By all accounts you are still sleeping with Dianne when you are in New York as well as Christine. My God, you are nothing but an oversexed lech, and so crude you make me sick.' She had gone too far...

For one timeless moment Theo looked capable of murder, his eyes darkening to black ice. 'Crude, am I? You don't know the meaning of the word, but perhaps it is time you learnt.' The menace in his tone cut through her anger and made her shiver in fear.

'No.' But she was too late. He hauled her close against his long body, his mouth crashing down on hers, forcing her lips apart in a kiss that was punishingly savage. He lifted his head, and tore the violet silk from her body to the hem, his black eyes skimming over her nakedness with a ruthlessness that terrified her. Then his lips found hers again and plundered the moist sweetness within, his hand curving her bottom, making her shockingly aware of his arousal.

'Make you sick, do I? And without the slightest effort he swung her up into his arms and dropped her on the bed, trapping her slender body beneath his own. 'Then I must do something about that.' She caught the implacable intent in his black eyes, and she did not have time to cry out before his mouth covered hers in a kiss that was as passionate as it was provocative.

Self-respect made her try to resist with all her strength, but it was no contest. He knew exactly what he was doing, how to wring a response from her. His hands were everywhere, caressing and stroking as he conducted a ravishment of her senses that had her sinking in a mindless sea of passion.

'No.' She found the will to cry out. 'No.' Her blue eyes were wild as he lifted his head and stared down at her.

'Oh, hell.' Theo groaned and rolled off the bed. He could not believe what he had almost done. Standing by the side of the bed, as he tied the belt of his robe, his eyes narrowed on her flushed face. 'You don't have to be afraid of me, Willow, not ever,' he said tautly.

'Don't flatter yourself. I am not.' Willow sat up and covered her nakedness with a sheet, her whole body throbbing with frustration.

'Don't lie. I saw it in your eyes,' he said, his face sardonic, 'and it stopped me cold. I would never hurt you, Willow. Though God knows you do your infuriating best to drive me mad.' He said it like a man at the end of his tether.

'Me drive you mad…?' She was almost speechless at the nerve of the man.

Theo stared for a long moment, and made a conscious effort to control his anger. Raging at her would get him nowhere, and his hard face softened in a smile of wry amusement. 'Yes, you witch…that is the kind of power you have, if you only knew it.' She was confused and it showed in the frown that marred her smooth brow.

'Come on, Willow.' He held out his hand to her. 'Let's go back to our room; this bed is too small for the two of us, and we can put tonight behind us. Forget about Christine, she never meant anything to me, and what we share together is so much better.'

Yes, sex and a son, Willow thought bitterly. Sex was his answer to everything, his arrogance monumental. He dismissed her arguments as nothing. Suddenly with blinding clarity she saw the future he had mapped out for her, a sexual slave kept in a gilded cage, pampered and petted as long as she asked no questions. Kept in her place, until all the vitality was drained out of her, and she ended up as little more than a cipher in his life. And Stephen—what kind of example as a woman would she be to him?

She rolled off the other side of the bed, and, dragging the sheet with her, she carefully wrapped it toga-style around her naked body. Finally taking a deep steadying breath, she turned to face Theo.

'You are an immoral, devious swine and I hate you,' she said bluntly, and there was no mistaking the cold determination in her face. 'Our marriage was a huge mistake, and much as I love Stephen I am not prepared to sacrifice my pride or my self-respect to pretend anything different. He is an intelligent boy and he would see through the farce in weeks.'

'Stephen apart, you could already be pregnant again—'

'I am not that big a fool,' she cut him off. 'I am on the pill courtesy of Anna's doctor. I don't make the same mistake twice.' Back stiff, she walked past him, her heart sick and aching, but not prepared to argue any more. Theo stood as though he had been turned to stone.

'And I actually thought I loved you,' she murmured with a negative shake of her head as she made for the door.

Theo flinched as though he had been struck, and desperately reached out for her, and swung her around to face him. 'What did you say?' he demanded hoarsely, his fingers shaking on her upper arms.

'You heard. It is over. Let go of me.'

'Not that, Willow.' He looked at her, his dark eyes gleaming with suppressed emotion. 'The part about thinking you love me.'

He had heard and her humiliation was complete. 'Past tense. *Thought.* I will be out of here in the morning and you can do your damnedest but you won't stop me.' She had to force the words out. It was hard because her throat was dry with unshed tears and she was hanging on to her self-control by a thread.

Theo stilled, his hands dropping from her shoulders, tension evident in every long line of his body. 'God, don't let it be too late,' he murmured under his breath, hectic colour burning up under his skin as he looked at her. It wasn't in his nature to be afraid but it took every scrap of courage he possessed to say, 'Please don't leave me, Willow. I love you. I think I always have.' He laid his heart on the line, and waited in an agony of suspense.

Willow thought she was hearing things. He towered over her, not a flicker of emotion apparent in his ruggedly handsome face, and the silence seemed to reverberate around the room. She raised her eyes to his and was stunned by the vulnerability in the dark depths that he could not quite hide.

She could not have been more shocked if he had hit her. She was conscious of the sudden erratic pounding of her heart as for a brief moment she was tempted to believe him. But fear of making a fool of herself all over again made her lash out.

'You expect me to believe that?' she said mockingly. 'I have just spent the evening with *your* mistress wearing the diamonds *you* gave her and discovered it is common knowledge you were going to marry her.' Surely not even Theo would stoop so low as to lie about being in love to keep her with him.

'I am telling you the truth, damn it.' Theo winced at the strength of his emotions, his firm lips twisting bitterly at the irony of the situation. The one and only time in his life he had told a woman he loved her, and she did not believe him. 'I admit Christine was my mistress, but I abandoned any thought of continuing the relationship as soon as I saw you again in London.'

'But you were going to marry her?'

His dark face tightened. 'The thought had crossed my mind. I wanted a child, but I sure as hell never proposed to her, whatever you may have heard.'

'Only because you found you had a ready-made son with me,' Willow countered. Deep inside she wanted to believe his avowal of love but she was determined not to be conned again.

'Damn it *agape mou!* What do I have to do to convince you?' he demanded, any trace of vulnerability vanishing as his expression changed to one of frustrated cynicism. 'I met you when you were a teenager and I retained a vivid memory of a beautiful girl who caught fire in my arms, and fulfilled my every desire. Only to discover the next morning

you had run away from me. I have told you all this before,'
he declared, shooting her a dark glance. 'I don't deny there
have been other women since, even a wife. I'm not a monk
and nine years is a long time. But they were all the same:
I provided them with a wealthy lifestyle and they provided
me with sex.

'The same as me, then,' she said flatly.

'No.' Theo put an arm around her slowly, as if afraid
she would push him away. 'Never think that. You are different,' he told her huskily as he gently brushed his fingers
over her cheek. His dark eyes burned down into hers, so
she had to look away, afraid of what he might make her
believe, make her feel.

'Yes, different because I had your son,' she countered
swiftly and wrenched out of his arms.

'No,' he denied adamantly, frustration getting the better
of him. Willow had already admitted without realising that
he had been her one and only lover, so she had to at least
care for him, even if she did not love him. He could live
with that. It was persuading Willow to do the same that
was his problem. He reached for her again, raking not quite
steady hands through her glorious hair as he cupped her
head and tilted her face up to his so she had to look at him.
He was fighting for his life here, and he had never been
more afraid.

'No, not because of Stephanos. But because for years I
carried the image of you in my head and heart. A bewitch-
ing black-haired creature. Sometimes in my worst moments
I thought I had imagined you, and your perfection was a
dream. And then I saw you again at the hotel, and it was
the same all over again.' He closed his eyes for a brief
moment and when he opened them the flame of possessive
passion in the black depths transfixed Willow.

'I looked at you and I wanted you, and I knew that I

would move heaven and earth to get you back, and this time for good. And before you say it again…not because of Stephanos, because at the time I did not know you had a child.'

Willow's eyes widened on his. He was right, he had wanted her without knowing about Stephen, and a slight ember of hope ignited in her heart.

'If you recall when we were alone in my suite I wanted to make love to you then, and if you are honest so did you,' he prompted, his hands dropping from her face to settle lightly on her shoulders. 'I could have persuaded you, but I didn't, because I felt I had rushed you the first time. I did not want to make the same mistake again and have you run away. I thought we had all the time in the world,' he said with a shake of his head. 'Much good my restraint did me. You still ran off like a thief in the night.' He was right again, she had run away, and suddenly his eyes, burning with a fire he made no attempt to hide, seared into hers. 'Do you have the slightest notion of how badly I want you?'

'Not really,' she whispered, her mouth dry. Some of her uncertainty must have shown in her face because he smiled down at her, the grim smile of a man under intense pressure.

'No, you probably don't,' he said gently. 'You were so young when we first met…too young. But when you left me I thought I was not quite a man because I ached for you so much. For my sins I even married another woman to try and forget you but still your image haunted my dreams. In the end finding Dianne in bed with another man was a relief—it gave me an excuse to divorce her.'

'But I thought—'

He cut her off before she could finish. 'Oh, I know what you thought; you laughed when I told you on our wedding night. But I have only myself to blame. It is what almost everyone else thinks as well. I allowed the rumours to circulate about another woman—some thought it was Christine—and I did nothing to disillusion them and I got a no-fault divorce.'

'That's what Charles said.' She agreed with him again.

His mouth twisted in a self-derisory smile. 'A sop to my ego.'

'That is so chauvinistic,' she declared in horror.

His dark brows rose. 'Oh, Willow, you are so naive,' he taunted and his hands drew her closer. 'A man is just as vulnerable as a woman, and in matters of sex probably more so.'

'Wait a minute,' she cried as a horrendous thought struck her. 'Did you sleep with Christine because Dianne slept with another man?' she asked. Her disgust was clear to see in her expressive eyes.

'No,' he breathed, his dark eyes gleaming with outrage. 'Are you determined to misunderstand everything I say?'

Willow took a deep unsteady breath and managed to keep her voice cool with the greatest difficulty. 'Well, that is what it sounded like to me.'

'If you knew me at all then you would know I would never use a woman that way.' His hands tightened over her shoulders. 'I swear I never slept with Christine until over two years after the divorce. Before that we were just friends and nothing more.'

'So you say,' she snorted.

'When have I ever given you reason to think so badly of me?' Theo demanded with barely leashed fury. 'You're my wife, the mother of my son, you belong to me.' His eyes darkened bitterly.

'Damn it, Willow.' He swore. 'I know I have made mistakes—this house, for a start. But the journalist in that magazine got it wrong—I did not build it for Dianne. It was a present from my father when I was twenty-five. The whole magazine story was Dianne's idea after Christine finished decorating the place for her. You were right about that, but all you had to do was tell me you didn't like it, instead of being so damn secretive. You can rip the place apart for all I care. I have already bought a small private island in the Aegean. The architect is drawing up plans for our house as we speak, and you will be the first to approve them. Is it too much to ask for a little trust?' he demanded roughly.

He had bought an island and was building them a house; Willow studied him with wide, wondering eyes, unable to think of a word to say.

'I swear I have not touched my ex-wife since the divorce and I have never touched another woman since the moment you walked down the stairs in the hotel, and back into my life,' Theo continued, completely misreading her silence and incensed by what he saw as her stubborn belief in his womanising ways. 'I have explained about Christine, damn it! And I'm sorry if you were hurt. I love you... What more do you want from me? Just tell me and it is yours.'

The breath caught in her throat as she saw the naked vulnerability and the pleading in his gleaming black eyes. The small ember of hope in her heart burned into a glorious flame. When she had met Theo again she had told him, *'I try never to dwell on the past but prefer to look to the future.'* Maybe now was the time to take her own advice and try to forget their past and put her trust in the future he was offering. 'Say that again?' she said softly.

Theo's devastatingly handsome features clenched in a frown. 'What...?' She infuriated and confused him, enraged him even.

Sometimes it was necessary to take a leap in the dark instead of always procrastinating and Willow realised that this was one such moment. 'That you love me, of course.' Instinctively she placed her trembling hands on his broad chest, feeling the thunderous pounding of his heart under her palms, and held her breath.

'Love you?' he launched back at her. 'I love you so much I can't live without you,' he affirmed, his black eyes glittering intently on her sparkling blue. 'I can't let you go, Willow,' he declared with savage determination. 'Not in eight years, not ever, and if that is selfish of me, so be it.'

'I have heard better ways of declaring one's love.' She smiled brilliantly at him, and slipped her hands up and around his neck. 'How about I will love you until the sea runs dry?' she suggested. 'Or until the stars cease to shine? Or maybe until the moon loses its glow?'

Theo's arms tightened around her convulsively. 'If that is what you want,' he said slowly, completely confused by her attitude. At least she was in his arms and smiling at him, which was a vast improvement on the past few hours.

'I don't know.' She looked at him through her lowered lashes. 'Perhaps something more like, until the universe implodes,' she teased, a tiny secret smile curving her luscious lips as she swayed into him. 'Or perhaps best of all…' she paused dramatically for a long moment '…I love you, Theo. Four words, simple and concise.'

With a throaty growl, Theo swept her up in his arms and, tripping over the end of the sheet that was wrapped haphazardly around her, he tumbled them onto the bed and all the breath was knocked out of her.

'You little witch—you love me,' Theo declared, his glorious dark eyes gleaming down into hers, and she nodded, too breathless to speak.

'Thank God! I think I have loved you from the first moment I saw you. But in my wildest dreams I never imagined you could feel the same way. You have no idea how often over the years I have wanted to come looking for you. But I told myself there was no such thing as love, especially at first sight. I want to be honest with you,' he said, suddenly serious. 'I was a complete cynic. A marriage for business, and, yes, perhaps for children, I could understand.' He gave a wry grimace. 'But love did not enter the equation as far as I was concerned. It was only tonight, when I was forced to face the prospect of losing you, that my head finally accepted what my heart has always known, and I was terrified.'

'It didn't stop you, though.' Willow reached up her hand and traced the strong line of his jaw in a loving gesture. He was a proud, arrogant man and he was hers.

'Where you're concerned nothing will ever stop me loving you,' he vowed, his heart and soul in his eyes as he leant over her and kissed her with an exquisite, possessive tenderness that told her better than any words he truly loved her. And the small bed proved more than adequate for the rest of the night.

But not so convenient the next morning when she woke enfolded in Theo's arms. He nuzzled her neck and murmured, 'So what was all that about using me as a serial killer in your first book?'

She tried to wriggle free but there was nowhere to go. 'I was hoping you had forgotten about that.' She raised laughing eyes up to his.

'I never forget anything about you, surely you know that by now.' He kissed her with breathtaking tenderness, and, lifting his head, he smiled. 'Did you really dislike me so much you had to have me killed off?' he prompted with a chuckle, but his dark eyes were oddly guarded, and Willow realised her arrogant husband was nowhere near as amused as he appeared.

'Dislike you, no, but to dismiss you from my mind, yes,'

she said honestly. 'I started writing that book when Stephen was a year old, and I was just beginning to get over the grief and pain of the past two years. I knew I had to get on with my life, but I wasn't sure how.'

'God, I wish I had been there for you.'

'Well, in a way you were. I didn't realise as I wrote the book that my villain bore a striking resemblance to you. A psychiatrist would probably have a field-day discerning my motive. I think killing you off in fiction acted like a catharsis, and I was able to move on with my life in a much happier state of mind.' Willow looped her arms around his neck. 'In fact you could say my success as a writer is really all down to you, Theo,' she declared with a brilliant smile.

'Thanks, I think,' Theo said with a rueful shake of his dark head. 'I don't know how you do it but you can make me believe anything.' And his hands stroked the lustrous black hair back from her face, his dark eyes gleaming with amusement. 'But no more using me in your books.' His hand, on the move again, stroked down her throat and lower to cup her breast. 'Or I might have to take serious measures to stop you.'

Willow's hands caressed down his back, and as she looked up into his face her blue eyes sparkled with mischief. 'Now that is a pity. I was thinking of incorporating romance into my next manuscript—my publisher tells me sex sells.' She trailed a finger down his spine, and felt him shudder. 'And as my only experience is with you, and you say I can't use you...' She paused to press a soft kiss on his broad, tanned shoulder. 'It's going to be hard, but I will have to find someone else to practise my fictitious sexual moves on.' She sighed theatrically.

Theo gave a shout of laughter and his hand tightened in her hair, his intent clearly written on his face, and in the depths of his glorious eyes. 'I already am hard, and you are not practising your moves on anyone else but me, from now to eternity. Is that imaginative enough for you?' he husked.

Willow smiled as his mouth claimed hers… And it was…

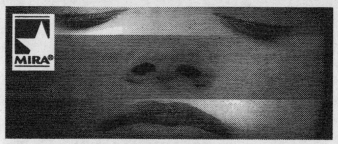

"Twisted villains, dangerous secrets...irresistible."
—*Booklist*

New York Times Bestselling Author

STELLA CAMERON

Just weeks after inheriting Rosebank, a once-magnificent Louisiana plantation, David Patin was killed in a mysterious fire, leaving his daughter, Vivian, almost bankrupt. With few options remaining, Vivian decides to restore the family fortunes by turning Rosebank into a resort hotel.

Vivan's dream becomes a nightmare when she finds the family's lawyer dead on the sprawling grounds of the estate. Suddenly Vivian begins to wonder if her father's death was really an accident...and if the entire Patin family is marked for murder.

Rosebank is not in Sheriff Spike Devol's jurisdiction, but Vivian, fed up with the corrupt local police, asks him for unofficial help. The instant attraction between them leaves Spike reluctant to get involved—until another shocking murder occurs and it seems that Vivian will be the next victim.

kiss them goodbye

"Cameron returns to the wonderfully atmospheric Louisiana setting...for her latest sexy-gritty, compellingly readable tale of romantic suspense."—*Booklist*

*Available the first week of October 2004,
wherever paperbacks are sold!*

If you enjoyed what you just read,
then we've got an offer you can't resist!

Take 2 bestselling love stories FREE!

Plus get a FREE surprise gift!

The world's bestselling romance series.

HARLEQUIN®
Presents

Seduction and Passion Guaranteed!

THEPRINCESSBRIDES

For duty, for money...for passion!

Discover a thrilling new trilogy from a rising star of Harlequin Presents®, Jane Porter!

Meet the Royals...

Chantal, Nicolette and Joelle are members of the blue-blooded Ducasse family. Step inside their sophisticated and glamorous world and watch as these beautiful princesses find they have to marry three international playboys—for duty, for money... and definitely for passion!

Don't miss

THE SULTAN'S BOUGHT BRIDE (#2418)
September 2004

THE GREEK'S ROYAL MISTRESS (#2424)
October 2004

THE ITALIAN'S VIRGIN PRINCESS (#2430)
November 2004

Pick up a Harlequin Presents® novel and you will enter a world of spine-tingling passion and provocative, tantalizing romance!

Available wherever Harlequin books are sold.

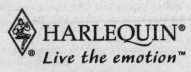

HARLEQUIN®
Live the emotion™

www.eHarlequin.com